I0532645

Broken

Matthew Storm

Copyright © 2013 Cranberry Lane Press

All rights reserved.

Follow Matthew on Twitter: @mjstorm

This is a work of fiction. Names, characters, places, and incidents
either are the product of the author's imagination or are used
fictitiously, and any resemblance to actual persons, living or dead,
business establishments, events, or locales is entirely coincidental.
The publisher does not have any control over and does not assume
responsibility for author or third-party websites or their content.

1st Edition

ISBN: 0692335617
ISBN-13: 978-0692335611

For Jalanie

Thank you

ACKNOWLEDGMENTS

Thanks to Michele, who read my very early drafts and didn't stop speaking to me as a result.

Also to Robert B. Parker and Lawrence Block, whose influence here will be evident.

Chapter 1

I don't know how long I lay in my bed listening to the wind chimes before I realized they weren't wind chimes at all, but the sound of my doorbell ringing. Nobody had rung my doorbell in quite some time and I'd forgotten what it sounded like. I didn't get a lot of visitors.

Who could be at the door? A particularly aggressive bill collector, maybe? That was awfully ambitious of them. It would also be fruitless. I didn't have any money in the house to give anyone, and there was very little anyone could threaten me with anymore.

I considered ignoring the bell, but the noise was interspersed with knocking now. Whoever was out there was not going to give up. I groaned and looked over at my bedside clock. It was 10:42 am. But on what day? The last day I had been aware of had been Thursday, but my blackouts were getting longer and longer these days, lasting upwards of a week sometimes. That made it hard to say for sure. Not that it really mattered. I didn't have a job and it wasn't like I had any place I needed to be.

The doorbell rang again and I finally gave up. I hauled myself out of bed and noticed that my legs were already beginning to tremble. That wasn't a good sign this early in the morning. A small glass tumbler sat on the bedside table, half full of clear liquid. I reached for it and took a sip, hoping that I hadn't gone crazy during the night and poured myself a glass of water. It was vodka, thank god. I downed the glass. The rush of alcohol hitting my stomach made me choke, and then I had to spend a minute swallowing hard to suppress my gag reflex to keep myself from throwing up. As long as I could keep it down, the vodka would keep withdrawal at bay for a little while.

I'd blacked out in street clothes, dirty jeans and an old t-shirt. At least I didn't need to get dressed. That would save me a minute of listening to that damn doorbell. I frowned, noticing I was only wearing one tennis shoe. What had happened to the other one? I pried the shoe off of my foot so I wouldn't be forced to limp around the house. I could find its mate later.

My bedroom floor was a forest of empty vodka bottles littered with fast-food wrappers I hadn't bothered to throw away. I tended not to worry about trash until insects started showing up in my house, and even then I was rarely sober enough to worry about it all that much. I started for the bedroom door, carefully picking my way through the mess. If I fell down in this condition, I wasn't going to be getting up again for quite a while.

The living room was in no better shape than the bedroom. The piles of garbage were bad enough, but worse was a sour smell that lingered in the air. It had to be something rotting, or maybe I had vomited on the carpet recently and failed to clean it up? That also would have done it. Later on I'd open a window up and get some fresh air into the place. That would help, at least a little bit.

The person outside was knocking again. "God damn it!" I snarled. The police department had taken my gun away when they'd fired me, but I could find another way to make whoever was out there wish they'd spent their morning bothering somebody else.

I made it to the door and opened it without bothering to look through the peephole. A tall, grey-haired man stood on the other side. He wore a dark suit that had never seen the rack and shoes that looked like they'd been shined two minutes before he'd started ringing my bell. The man smiled pleasantly at me. "Nevada James?"

"I gave at the office," I said.

A puzzled expression crossed the man's face. "Gave what?"

"Never mind," I said. I was never funny first thing in the morning. "What do you want?"

"My name is Chandler Emerson," the man said, extending a hand to shake. It was difficult not to notice his perfect manicure. He was definitely not a bill collector, then. I didn't offer him my hand, anyway. He held his own in the air for a moment, then dropped it back to his side as casually as if he'd never made the gesture.

"What do you want?" I repeated.

"I represent Alan…" he began, but then his face suddenly wrinkled and he took a step back. The smell had hit him, then, either my own or whatever was stinking up the inside of my house. I wasn't sure when I had last changed clothes, but I probably hadn't showered in even longer. I didn't much care how I smelled. It wasn't as if I had a social life. I only left the house for food and alcohol.

"You were saying?" I asked.

Emerson cleared his throat. "I was saying, I represent Alan Davies." He looked at me expectantly, as if I was supposed to be impressed with this information.

I thought about it for a moment. I'd heard that name before, hadn't I? Was it someone I had borrowed money from? No, I'd probably be able to remember that. But then I placed him. "Alan Davies? The Mafia guy?" What the hell could Alan Davies possibly want with *me*?

Emerson scowled. "Mr. Davies is a well-respected businessman, and scurrilous accusations like that…"

"Oh, I don't give a shit," I interrupted. "I'm not a cop anymore. You said you represent him. You're his lawyer?"

"Yes."

"Why are you here?"

I saw Emerson's lips tighten into a thin line. "Mr. Davies has a business proposition he would like to discuss with you. I have come to convey you to his estate."

I looked toward the street and saw a black Lincoln town car parked at the curb. A muscular man in a grey chauffeur's uniform stood waiting next to an open rear door. He even wore a jaunty little cap to complete the outfit, but I was more interested in the bulge I could see in the left side of his jacket. He was either carrying a pistol or his lunch under there, and he didn't look all that hungry.

"Some people call," I told Emerson.

"Mr. Davies felt that would be impersonal, and asked me to come myself in order to convey his respect for you."

I stifled a laugh. I had no idea what Alan Davies looked like, but it was hard not to imagine Marlon Brando when Emerson talked like that. "So I'm supposed to get in there and take a ride with you?" I asked.

"Indeed."

I shook my head. "Look, I don't know what your boss is thinking, but I didn't switch teams when the cops fired me. I don't do jobs for gangsters. Tell him to fuck off."

"The proposition Mr. Davies wishes to discuss with you is entirely legal," Emerson said primly. "I can assure you that none of your ethics will be compromised."

"Get lost." I started to close the door on him.

"Mr. Davies will pay you ten thousand dollars simply to meet with him," Emerson said quickly.

I hesitated for a moment, then opened the door again. "You're serious?" I asked him. "Ten grand?"

"Ten thousand dollars," Emerson repeated, looking annoyed. "Cash. If you don't care for what he has to say, you can walk away, and the money is yours to keep."

"He'll let me just walk off with ten grand, and I don't have to do anything but listen to him? Why am I having trouble believing that?"

"He gives you his solemn word."

I thought it over. Alan Davies's solemn word didn't mean a

lot to me, but ten thousand dollars would pay a lot of bills, and I was behind on my rent and…I was behind on *everything*.

"He's wasting his time if he asks me to do anything illegal," I said. "Don't give me that legitimate businessman shit."

"Nothing illegal," Emerson said.

I frowned. "He knows I didn't work organized crime? If he wants to know what the cops have on him, I have no idea, and I wouldn't tell him even if I did."

Emerson opened his mouth and I could tell he was about to deny what Alan Davies did for a living again. I cocked my head at him and he caught himself. "Mr. Davies knows you were a homicide detective. He will not ask you for any information with regards to your former employer."

I shrugged. "Fine. Let's go."

Emerson pursed his lips, looking at me skeptically. "Perhaps you'd like to…"

"What?"

"Bathe?" he suggested. "And change clothes, perhaps?"

I looked down at my t-shirt. I really had been wearing it for quite a while. It was stained with things I didn't particularly want to think about. I should probably change it before it rotted and fell off. Maybe I'd even stick it in the washing machine. "All right," I told Emerson. "You can wait out here." Even if I had been in the habit of inviting Mafia lawyers into my house, it probably would have been a good idea to clean the place up a little first. I wasn't sure Emerson would have been able to handle the smell.

"I'll wait in the car," Emerson said, looking just a bit

relieved. "See you soon, Ms. James."

Chapter 2

We left my small Ocean Beach house half an hour later and were quickly heading north on I-5, away from San Diego. I'd showered and changed into another pair of jeans and a t-shirt I'd chosen because it stank less than anything else lying on my bedroom floor. I really did need to do laundry soon. Maybe I'd get really ambitious and put away the clothes once they were clean. Well, I probably wouldn't, but it's fun to pretend.

After a few minutes on the freeway I nodded off, waking up only when I felt the car pull to a stop. We were at a tall metal security gate in what could only have been an extremely upscale neighborhood. Our chauffeur rolled down his window and spoke to a security guard who had walked up to the car. This guard had a bulge under his jacket, as well. Another concealed weapon, then, but his was bigger than the driver's, and too bulky to be an ordinary pistol. I wondered what he was carrying under there. Something that could fire a lot of bullets in a short amount of time, I was guessing.

"Where are we?" I asked. My voice was scratchy and my

mouth tasted like something had crawled in there and died. I wished I'd remembered to brush my teeth when I'd been cleaning up earlier, or at least brought along some mints.

Emerson gave me a sidelong glance, barely concealed disgust in his eyes. "Solana Beach."

I knew the area, although I'd never spent much time up here. Solana Beach was nestled on the Pacific coast between Del Mar and Cardiff-by-the-Sea, about half an hour north of San Diego. Houses up here could easily cost more than I'd have ever made in my entire career as a cop. It was an area where movie stars and hedge fund managers lived. I wondered if any of them knew they had a gangster for a neighbor.

"Drug business pays pretty good, huh?" I asked Emerson.

He glared at me. "Mr. Davies is not…" he stopped the sentence short as I raised my eyebrows at him. "Never mind," he said, looking away.

I smirked. "Problem?"

Emerson looked back at me as the security gate rolled open and we passed through. "I was given instructions to bring you to Mr. Davies," he explained. "If that hadn't been the case, I would have left you where I found you. This will be a short meeting. You're clearly in no condition to be of any use to anyone."

He was right, of course, but I pouted anyway. "Aw," I said. "You don't like me?"

"No."

"I like *you*," I said.

His eyes widened just a bit. "You do?"

"No," I said. "Not really."

Emerson sighed and went back to looking out the window. "Waste of time," he muttered to himself, just loudly enough for me to hear.

Alan Davies lived in a white Greek Revival house, although *house* didn't seem like the right word in this case. *Monstrosity* would have been better. It was of a type that had been popular in the 1980's among people who had too much money and far too little taste, although I'd never seen the design carried out on this scale before. It was easily the biggest house I had ever seen, and probably cost more than a mid-sized Gulfstream jet.

"Good *god*," I marveled at it. "How many rooms are in that thing?"

Emerson allowed himself a small, satisfied smile. "Forty-seven. It's impressive, isn't it?"

"I was going to say *grotesque*, but that's close enough."

He sniffed. "I wouldn't expect you to have any experience of the finer things, having had to make do on your police officer's salary."

I looked over at him. "I hope I don't remember my police officer's training," I said. "I might start asking questions about where your boss got the money to pay for that thing."

Emerson turned to me, anger flashing in his eyes. He opened his mouth to speak but I cut him off before he could start. "Fucking threaten me," I said. My voice had an edge in it I hadn't heard in quite some time, and I was secretly pleased that I could still summon it when I wanted it. "Do it. You've read the papers. You know all about me. What do you think I'll do to you?"

I could tell he was thinking about it, but he looked into my eyes and didn't like what he saw there. Few people did. He shut his mouth. I thought about taunting him a little more, but I held my tongue. It wasn't his fault I'd been waking up on the wrong side of the bed for the last three years.

The driveway ran in a circle around a large marble fountain that I'd have been tempted to throw a handful of change into, if I'd had any change with me. Our chauffeur parked the town car at the point in the driveway closest to the mansion's front doors. Emerson got out of the car as the chauffeur came around and held my door open for me. I wished I'd brought sunglasses along. It was a bright, cloudless day, and while I was well past the point in my drinking of waking up with hangovers, the sunlight didn't feel good. It made me feel like a vampire caught in the center of a football field at noon.

I hauled myself out of the car and took stock of my surroundings. I could see at least six armed guards patrolling the grounds. Each carried an MP5 submachine gun. I was no expert on assault weapons but I recognized those easily. The MP5 was one of the most popular guns in the world, at least among militaries and law enforcement agencies. They were also highly illegal in California, unless the laws had been changed in the last few years. I hadn't really been paying attention, to be honest.

"Looks like you're expecting someone to storm the place," I said. "You think someone is going to try and reenact the end of *Scarface* up here?"

"One can never be too careful, Ms. James," Emerson said. "This way, please." I was disappointed that he hadn't said "walk this way" so I'd have had an excuse to imitate him. I was even more disappointed when he began walking toward a gazebo located in the center of an immaculate lawn about fifty yards away.

"We're not going into the house?" I asked. Aside from getting out of the sun, I'd been hoping for a chance to make fun of Davies's furniture. God only knew what kind of crap he had in there.

Emerson looked at me as if I'd suggested we drag a dead goat into the foyer together. "We are not," he said. "Mr. Davies is this way."

I wasn't thrilled about the walk but I followed as Emerson led me across the lawn. I had enough booze in my system to keep the shakes at bay, but my legs were unsteady and this was more exertion than I was accustomed to in the morning. When we were halfway to the gazebo I felt myself starting to sweat, and I knew it wasn't from the heat.

A round glass table sat in the center of the gazebo with places set for two people. An assortment of pastries and fruit had been laid out, but I was more interested in the crystal pitcher and two champagne glasses I saw. They looked to be filled with orange juice, and if I was lucky, champagne.

A man in his forties with thick salt and pepper hair stood next to the table. He was solidly built but not fat, with a barrel chest and a weight-lifter's arms. He wore shorts that went down to his knees and a Tommy Bahama shirt. *Island lifestyles for the casual drug lord*, I thought.

He extended his hand as I stepped into the gazebo. "Alan Davies," he smiled. "Thank you for coming, Ms. James."

I ignored his hand. "Ten thousand dollars gets you a meeting," I said. "That's it."

He withdrew his hand but the warm smile stayed on his face. "Won't you sit down?" he made a sweeping gesture at the table.

I sat, reaching for the champagne glass closest to me. As I'd hoped, it was a mimosa. I downed half of it in one swallow and sighed in contentment. Either it was very good champagne, or I'd desperately needed it. Probably a little of both. "Where's the money?" I asked.

Davies sat down across from me, nodding at a leather briefcase adjacent to the table. "Ten thousand dollars, as promised. Would you like to count it before we begin?"

I chuckled. "You must be out of your damn mind," I told Davies. "Ten grand to sit here with you? Why did you call me up here?"

"I have a problem," he said, sipping his own mimosa. "I was told that you might be able to help me with it."

"Oh, yeah? Who told you that?"

"Dan Evans."

That got my attention. Dan was a captain in the San Diego Police Department's homicide division. He had been my boss back when I was a detective, and he was quite possibly my only friend. I hadn't seen him in quite a while, though. The last time we'd spoken...well, the last time we'd spoken I'd threatened to kill him if I ever saw him again. I had been roaring drunk at the time, but that wasn't much of an excuse for the way I'd behaved.

"Won't you eat something?" Davies asked. "The fruit came from the farmer's market this morning. Please, help yourself."

I had no idea when I'd eaten last, but these days I had

trouble keeping anything solid down for long. My drinking problem doubled as a pretty effective weight-loss plan. "I'm fine," I said. "How do you know Dan? I would think gangsters and cops don't generally travel in the same social circles."

Emerson, who had taken a standing position a few feet behind his boss, stiffened visibly at the "gangster" comment, but Davies didn't flinch. "We grew up in the same neighborhood in El Cajon."

"You're kidding me?" Dan had never mentioned that when we'd been on the force together, but I supposed it wasn't quite the same thing as saying you went to high school with Bono or Barack Obama.

"We weren't especially close," Davies said. "Don't get me wrong. But I always thought he was a good man and when I went to him for help, he gave me your name."

"He *recommended* me? Seriously?"

"Yes."

"Then he was fucking with you," I said. "You may not have noticed this, but," I held up my glass so he could see it and then downed the second half of my mimosa as he watched. "I'm in no condition to help anyone," I finished.

"You're very frank," he mused as I refilled my glass from the pitcher on the table. The mimosas were great, but I failed to see the need for all the orange juice. It was just wasting space in the glass.

"That's because I don't give a shit anymore," I said.

Davies studied my face. "Your confrontation with the Laughing Man was…"

I pointed at him. "Don't ever say that name to me."

He nodded. "Excuse me, then. Your last case was the subject of much media interest, of course, as was your subsequent breakdown and dismissal from the police force. I knew all of that. Dan told me that things had…*deteriorated*…for you since then. I admit he didn't tell me it was…" he motioned at my half-empty second mimosa. "He didn't say it was that bad."

"It's even worse than you think," I told him, nodding at Chandler Emerson. The lawyer had been smirking quietly at me. "Ask *him* what I looked like when he came to pick me up."

Davies glanced back at Emerson, who shook his head slowly, the smirk still on his face. "This has been the most expensive waste of time of your life," I informed Davies. "I do like the mimosas, though. Thanks."

Davies sighed and ate a strawberry, chewing it slowly as he thought. I knew he'd heard the stories about me. Nevada James, youngest woman ever to make detective in the SDPD. Nevada James, who cracked every case she was given. Nevada James, who had gone one-on-one with the Laughing Man, the most notorious serial killer in San Diego's history…and lost. Nevada James, who had been committed to a mental hospital, and who had been too unstable to keep her job once she was released. What on earth had Davies expected to find, I wondered. A hungry detective out to redeem herself? He must watch a lot of television. I almost felt sorry for the naïve twit.

I suppose I should have felt sorry for *me*, but the alcohol helped with that.

"Dan Evans tells me you are the finest investigator he has ever met," Davies said.

I shrugged. "I'm modest, but yeah. I was." I frowned thoughtfully. "Oh, I guess that wasn't very modest at all, was it?"

"My wife and daughter are missing," Davies said abruptly.

I nearly spilled my second mimosa. "Jesus Christ," I laughed. "Are you serious with this?"

"Yes," Davies said firmly.

I shook my head. "Look, you need to call the police, or the FBI, or, I don't know…" I motioned towards one of the armed guards he had patrolling the grounds. "Get your goons on it."

"*Goons?*"

"Do you people not say *goons* anymore?" I asked.

"Not since Prohibition."

"Oh."

"I think you know I can't go to law enforcement," he continued. "And as for getting my people involved…well, for all I know this isn't even a problem."

"How long have they been missing?"

"Ten days."

I stared at him. "Then how could it possibly not be a problem?"

"My wife and I are separated. She has her own condo in La Jolla. We share custody of Anna."

"Okay."

"Often when my wife…*wants* something…" he struggled to

find the right words. "She can be prone to dramatic gestures."

"Oh, really?"

"I would not be surprised if this were one of them." Davies spread his hands apart. "We had been arguing about money. She has very likely taken Anna and checked into a hotel for a few days to make a point."

"That sounds like something women do," I nodded. "I'm always going and checking into hotels at the first thing. I order a shitload of room service, too."

His lips tightened. "I know you're making fun of me, but she has done this kind of thing before."

"Fair enough. Then why are you so concerned about it this time?"

He sighed. "Ordinarily she'd call me to make threats. Tell me I'll never see my daughter again, that kind of thing. This time, not a word."

I poured myself another drink, wondering what my limit on mimosas was. Then I remembered I didn't believe in limits. "And what if I said I don't believe you?" I asked. "What if I said it's far more likely that you're an abusive criminal thug and you want me to track her down because she's hiding from you and you can't find her?"

"I'd say Dan Evans never would have given me your name if that was even a possibility," he replied.

I had to admit, he made a pretty good point. Dan was as upstanding a guy as you could find. He'd never have helped Davies if he thought he was hurting his wife or the child. He'd have slapped handcuffs on him and dragged him off to a holding cell.

17

"All right," I said. "So what is it you're asking me to do here? Find her and tell her to come home?"

"Not at all," he said. "Find them and confirm they're safe. That's all. Then report back to me."

"Oh, so you can send your goons to go get her?" Davies cocked his head at me like a confused dog. "I'm going to keep saying *goons*," I told him. "I like the way it sounds."

"You don't need to tell me where they are if you don't think it's appropriate," Davies said. "My wife will come home when she's ready. I just want you to confirm that they're safe. And the reason I don't send my…*goons*…is because I'm trying not to escalate things with her. Believe it or not, I'm the good guy here."

"Yeah, you seem like a pretty reasonable guy," I said.

"Thank you. I…" he peered at me. "You didn't mean that, did you?"

"No," I said.

He let out a long sigh. I tended to have that effect on people. "Will you help me?"

I considered it. Something wasn't sitting right with me. "Why don't you hire a private detective if you don't want to use your own people?"

Emerson cleared his throat loudly. Davies gave him an annoyed glance, then looked back at me. "He's fun," I said to Davies. "Chandler Emerson. Did you go through the phone book and pick the lawyer with the most pretentious name? You had to figure he was good, with a name like that."

"Chandler is an excellent attorney," Davies said. "But

despite his advice, I don't trust private detectives."

"Why not?"

"They're motivated by money."

"*I'm* motivated by money," I said. "Money got me up here, not the chance to ride in a Lincoln, as exciting as that may have been."

"But you are motivated by…" he looked at me carefully and I could see that he was debating with himself whether he should cross a line. "My daughter is a ten-year-old girl. She may be in danger. Will you help her?"

My hand tightened around my champagne glass and for a moment I thought I might accidentally break it. I sat it down slowly on the table and removed my hand, trying to keep it from trembling. This time the shaking wasn't a symptom of withdrawal.

I took in a deep breath and let it out slowly. There was no way I was going to let Davies see me lose control. "Dan told you to say that, didn't he?"

"Yes," Davies admitted. He looked almost ashamed of himself.

I nodded. That would have been the only possible reason Davies would have known to say that. Dan had given him one of my triggers.

Dan would be getting a visit from me today. He wasn't going to enjoy it.

"I'll find your family," I said. "I won't tell you where they are if they don't want to be found."

"That's fi…" he began.

"No," I interrupted. "I'm going to check you out. If I even get a hint that you're lying to me, we're done, and you have a new enemy."

"I under…"

"No!" I interrupted again. "You *don't*. You don't know what that means. You're used to intimidating people. You're a big guy and in your little gangster world I'll bet you're pretty scary." I leaned forward and pointed at him. "You don't ever want to imagine that I'm afraid of you. After what I've gone up against, you're a…you're a fucking *pedestrian*. Do you understand me? I don't give a shit about you."

That had been more words then I'd spoken all at once in weeks. I was a little bit proud of myself.

Davies looked uncertain of what to say to that. He bit his lip. "I don't think anyone has ever spoken to me that way," he said.

I shrugged. I could already see that he wasn't going to make a move on me. I almost wished he would. I'd never get out of here alive, not in my condition, not surrounded by so many men with guns, but that didn't bother me. I'd been living with death for a long time. This was as good a day as any.

"I accept your terms," Davies said. "Find my family and do whatever you think is appropriate with the information."

"Fine," I said. "Money."

He motioned to the briefcase next to the table. "Ten thousand dollars."

"That bought you a conversation," I told him. "That's all."

Chandler Emerson took a step forward to protest but

Davies held up a hand and he stopped in his tracks. "Five more," Davies said.

"Fifteen," I said. "No, twenty. Make it thirty thousand all together."

"Thirty thousand dollars?" Davies asked, eyes wide.

"It's nothing to you," I said. "Look at what you spent on that thing you call a house."

Emerson looked like he was about to have a seizure, but Davies hesitated only a fraction of a second. "Done. Thirty thousand."

That had been easy. I should have asked for fifty. But I had no right to complain. Thirty thousand dollars would keep the bill collectors off my back for a very long time. Probably longer than I'd live, given the questionable state of my health these days.

"I'll need information," I said. "Legal name, her address in La Jolla, names of friends. Whatever you can tell me."

"Chandler has prepared a dossier for you." I snickered. "What?" Davies asked.

"*Dossier.*"

"It's a word," Davies said. "People say it."

"When they're telling James Bond where to go, sure they do."

"Fine," he said. "We have some *papers* for you to look at."

"That'll work."

"How long do you think it will take you to find anything?"

"I have no idea," I admitted. "I was a homicide detective.

21

I've never done a missing persons case."

"So…" Davies raised his eyebrows hopefully. "A few days?"

"Maybe. I'll call you."

"Please let me know the minute you have something." He reached into his shirt pocket and pulled out a business card. "That number will work for the rest of the week," he said, handing it to me.

I looked at the card. It had a handwritten telephone number on it, and nothing else. I recognized the area code. "That's a cell phone in New Jersey," I said.

"The rest of the week," he repeated, patting a small bulge in his shirt pocket where I assumed the corresponding cell phone was tucked away. They were using disposable phones, of course. Probably picked them up in a 7-11, used them for a few days, and then tossed them into the ocean. But shipping them across the country first? That was a new one for me.

"Todd will drive you home," Davies said. "Can I assume you'll start right away?"

"Todd?" I asked.

He nodded at the chauffeur who had driven me up here. The other man was now standing on the grass a few yards to my right. I hadn't seen him approaching. Booze really had dulled my senses. In the old days, when I was on my game, he'd never have gotten within twenty yards of me without my knowing about it.

I stood up and took the briefcase from next to the table. It felt nice and heavy. Later I'd have to take the cash out and look at it. I had no idea what ten thousand dollars looked like.

Maybe I'd throw the bills up in the air and make it rain. "Home first," I said, "then I have to make another stop."

"He can take you to La Jolla to have a look at her condo, if you like?"

"No," I said. "I have to go see an old friend first"

"Who's that?"

I looked at Davies, my expression hard. "Oh," he said, nodding. "Well, tell Dan I said thanks for his help."

"I'm going to tell him a lot of things," I said. "I'm pretty sure 'thanks' isn't going to be one of them."

Chapter 3

I resolved to stay awake and pay attention to the route we were taking as Todd drove me away from Davies's estate. It was reasonable to assume that I'd need to come back here at some point. Not that I expected to be invited over to any gangster parties, but you never knew what was going to happen.

"Nevada James," Todd said.

I glanced up at him. He was staring straight ahead at the road. Had he meant to say that out loud?

"What?"

"That's a funny name."

"My parents were hippies."

"Oh."

I looked at the thin manila file folder Emerson had presented me with before I'd gotten into the car. I hadn't bothered to open it yet, but the name HEATHER DAVIES was written across the front in thick black pen. I didn't what constituted a *dossier* these days, but I imagined I wouldn't find much more than the same information you'd get off of a driver's license. The folder wasn't thick enough to hold much else.

We turned onto the Pacific Coast Highway and I looked out at the ocean for a few minutes as we drove south. I could make out people wading in the water near the shore, and farther out a few surfers were trying their luck. San Diego wasn't known for great waves, but people did get lucky now and then.

I looked back at Todd. He was still staring ahead at the road, eyes fixed as if he expected it to disappear at any moment. "Nice day," he said.

That was Todd's second attempt at small talk, but his knuckles were white on the steering wheel and he hadn't turned his head or looked at me in the mirror either time he'd spoken. Why was he nervous? Either he was working up the nerve to ask me out, or…

"Any idea where I should start looking for her, Todd?"

"For Heather?"

For *Heather*. Not for Mrs. Davies. That was what I'd thought. "I'd love to know what you think about all of this," I said.

"Ma'am?" Now he *was* looking at me in the rearview mirror, but that wasn't curiosity I saw in his eyes. He knew he'd screwed up, but I doubted he knew exactly how.

"You guys were pretty close. What do you think is going on?"

"Close, ma'am?"

"You were sleeping with her. That seems pretty close to me."

"I wasn't…"

"Where's that number your boss gave me?" I asked, pretending to search my pockets. "I better call him."

Todd jerked the steering wheel to the right and we skidded to an abrupt stop on the side of the road. The first two cars to pass by us honked angrily. I watched Todd, trying to conceal my amusement. He was breathing hard now and his eyes were frantic. "You can't tell him. Please!"

"Tell me what's going on, Todd."

"Promise you won't tell him first. He'll kill me if he finds out."

I suppressed a sigh. This was going to be far too easy. At this rate I'd be collecting my fee and buying myself a magnum of something cold and dry by the end of the day. "I really couldn't give a shit, Todd. Tell me the truth and he'll never hear about it from me."

Todd sounded like he was about to hyperventilate. I waited for him to get himself back under control. I suppose I could have been more reassuring, but that had never been one of my strong points.

When he got his breathing under control Todd said, "We were just screwing around, you know?"

"Sure I do."

"She's…well, she's fucking *hot*, you know? And she wanted it. I knew it was a bad idea, but…"

"You couldn't help yourself?"

"Yeah. And even if I'd said no, Heather is pretty aggressive. She's used to getting what she wants."

"Women," I nodded. "I hear ya, Todd. Do you know where she is?"

"No."

"You two aren't running away together?"

"No."

"I don't care, don't get me wrong. But if I find you two shacked up in a motel room together after we've just had this conversation, I'm going to be pretty pissed, Todd. You don't want me to be pissed, do you?"

"I swear I have no idea where she is!"

I watched him sweat for a minute. "When was the last time you saw her?"

"Over a month ago."

I thought it over. "She broke it off with you?"

"Yeah. It was just a fling, you know? We weren't a couple."

"How did you feel about that?"

"Not great, but what was I going to do? Argue with her? She told me it was over, and if I made trouble for her, she'd tell her husband about it."

"And then you'd be sleeping with the fishes."

He looked at me in the mirror, confused. "What?"

"Sleeping with the fishes. What, you've never heard that one before?"

"Once. On television. I never heard anyone say it in real

life."

"Next you'll be telling me you never heard anyone say *goons*, either."

He frowned. "I haven't."

"It was rhetorical, Todd."

"Okay."

I had the idea Todd really didn't want me to ask him what *rhetorical* meant. "Do you have any idea where she'd go? A friend? A favorite vacation spot? A hotel?" Maybe Davies had been right and she was holed up in a resort somewhere, sipping margaritas and working on her tan.

Todd shook his head. "No. I don't think she has any real friends. Her parents are dead, as far as I know. She was a dancer when she met the boss, but I don't think she kept in touch with any of those people."

I sighed. Maybe I wouldn't be buying that magnum tonight, after all. It could wait. "Fine," I said. "Drive."

Todd looked back at me. "You won't say anything, will you?"

"No," I said. "Not unless I find out you lied to me."

"I didn't lie."

"Then you've got nothing to worry about."

Todd put the car back in gear and we pulled up outside my house twenty minutes later. It wasn't my house, strictly speaking. I'd been renting it from an elderly couple in La Mesa since back when I'd been a police officer. I had no idea how far behind on the rent I was, but they'd never exercised their right to kick me out to the street. I imagined they must have felt sorry for me after watching me go from the SDPD's bright star to the train wreck I was now. And there was the fact that I'd helped them out, years ago, when their teenage delinquent son had gotten into some very serious trouble with some very serious people. They probably felt the need to go easy on me. Even so, I owed them a great deal of money and I intended to pay it very soon. I was sure they wouldn't mind taking the back rent in cash, and maybe I'd give them a few months extra in advance. I could afford it now.

I told Todd to wait for me and went inside to hide the briefcase of cash under my bed. That wasn't going to be enough to stop a determined thief, but any thief who had the stomach to make it past the smell in my living room without fainting deserved whatever he could find.

Todd had kept the car running and seemed to have calmed down considerably when I got back inside. "Where to?"

"Police headquarters," I said. "You know where it is?"

"Sure," he nodded.

"Yeah, of course you do." I imagined that given his line of work, he had almost certainly been there before.

SDPD headquarters was fifteen minutes away, in a building that looked like that Tetris block you don't want to get because it never fits in anywhere. It took up most of the city block on Broadway between 14th and 15th Avenues downtown, just a stone's throw from where I-5 snaked through the city.

Todd parallel parked in front of the building. "Here we are."

"Wait for me," I said.

"I'm not a taxi," he complained. "I have things to…"

"What's that?" I cupped my hand to my ear. "Did you say I don't need to be discreet anymore about that affair you had with Alan Davies's wife?"

Todd grunted. "Nothing."

"Damn right, nothing."

I stepped out of the car and took a good look at the building where I'd spent my entire adult career. How long had it been since I'd been back here? It had been three years since the Laughing Man. Two and a half since I'd gotten out of the hospital. And then I'd been back on the force just long enough to demonstrate I was too unstable to be a cop anymore. Two years, maybe, since they'd shown me the door for good.

It had been a long time, I thought. Two years ago I'd sworn I'd never set foot inside this building again. But as I looked at the building now, I had to admit a tiny part of me missed it. Wasn't this just a little bit like coming home after a long absence?

Maybe.

Then I leaned forward and vomited on the sidewalk.

Chapter 4

The retching was over pretty quickly. I had nothing solid in my stomach to get rid of. I was breathing hard when I finished and had to put a hand on the town car to steady myself as I got my stomach back under control. Todd didn't get out of the car to see if I was all right. Either he hadn't noticed the vomiting, or he was too annoyed with me to care. It didn't make all that much difference to me. This kind of thing happened all the time lately. I was more sorry to lose what was left of my mimosas than anything else.

When I felt reasonably steady again I started for the building's main entrance, ignoring the questioning looks from people on the sidewalk who had stopped to watch me be sick. The stares didn't bother me. Vomiting was hardly the most embarrassing thing I'd ever done in public.

There was a line at the building's entrance for the metal detector that anyone not wearing a badge had to go through. I passed through it without anyone giving me a second look. I didn't have anything interesting in my pockets, and I hadn't bothered to bring a purse along. It occurred to me that that meant I didn't have any identification, but I didn't think I'd be needing it any time soon.

My destination was on the 4th floor of the building. I'd have preferred to avoid a crowded elevator in case I got sick again. Throwing up on the sidewalk was one thing. Doing it in an elevator was quite another. But there was no way I was strong enough to get up four flights of stairs. My legs probably wouldn't start to shake for a few hours yet, but they felt weak and I'd already had a lot more exertion than usual today.

The Homicide Division was in a large open room filled with desks arranged in pairs. Offices for the higher-ranking officers lined the walls, giving each one a view of San Diego's downtown area. None of the offices were particularly large, and a corner office here certainly didn't have the cachet that a corner office in a Fortune 500 company would carry, but once upon a time an office had been all I wanted. Rank and power didn't mean anything to me, but views were priceless.

Nobody gave me a second look until I was halfway to my destination, and then the atmosphere in the room abruptly changed as I was noticed. Murmurs started up instantly and a few people rose from their desks. I was a legend here, but being a legend can carry as many bad things with it as it can good.

A pretty woman in her early thirties put herself directly in my path, forcing me to stop. I looked at her curiously, struggling to remember her name. Had we been friends?

The woman bit her lip nervously. "Nevada?" she asked. "Are you okay?"

"Sarah," I said, remembering her. Of course. Sarah Winters

had been new to Homicide when I'd gotten the Laughing Man case. She'd been there for the beginning of the end. I remembered her telling me I was her role model once. What a lousy judge of character she'd turned out to be.

"Yes, I'm Sarah," she said slowly, as if she was speaking to a lost tourist who didn't understand English. "Can you remember me?"

For a minute I didn't know what she was talking about, but then it occurred to me that she must think I'd gone off my meds and wandered in here by accident. It was a reasonable conclusion given that I'd once been locked up in a psych ward, but she was wrong about the meds. The only medication I'd ever been given in there were tranquilizers to stop my uncontrollable, hysterical laughter. At first. Later the same tranquilizers were used to stop me from screaming. After my stint in the ward I'd been mandated to see a psychiatrist, but I'd thrown the prescription he'd given me in the trash and never gone back.

"I'm fine, Sarah," I told her. "It's okay. I'm here to see Dan."

"Okay." She looked me up and down and I could see a blend of fear and sorrow in her eyes. Had some of the vomit splashed onto my clothes? "You look…" she began.

"Yeah?"

"You look really bad, Nevada."

I blinked in surprise. "Okay," I said. "Well, I appreciate your honesty, Sarah." I put a hand on her shoulder. "You need to get out of my way now."

"Nevada, I…"

I shook my head at her. I didn't begin to have time for this. "Sarah, I always liked you. You're a nice girl and I knew you'd make a good detective. But you need to get out of my way now." I didn't need to raise my voice. My tone didn't invite argument or discussion.

Sarah swallowed hard and stepped aside. I looked around the room. Every eye was fixed on me now. I'd known I couldn't walk around up here without drawing at least *some* attention, but I hadn't expected all of this. But then, the last time I'd been in this room it had ended pretty badly. If I hadn't been a cop, I probably would have gone to jail for what I'd done.

I made it to the northwest corner office without any further interruptions. Dan Evans, my former boss, was sitting behind his desk. He was a huge bear of a man whose dress shirts never fit him right and whose ties always seemed comically small on his frame. I'd offered to take him shopping more than once; the man needed some quality time in a Big & Tall department like nobody's business. He'd never taken me up on it.

Dan was talking with one of the higher-ups from Vice whose name I couldn't remember when I stepped into his office. "Get out," I said to the other man.

"Excuse me?" the Vice cop asked.

Dan raised a hand in a gesture of supplication. "It's all right, Harry," he said. "We can finish up later."

Harry, whoever he was, stood up and looked me square in the eyes. "You've got a lot of damn nerve coming back here."

"Do something about it," I dared him.

Harry eyed me for a second, then glanced back at Dan.

"You need me to call someone?"

"No," Dan said. "Don't. Do me a favor and shut the door on your way out."

Harry took another look at me as he passed by, closing the door behind him. I turned my attention to Dan. He gave me a small half-smile. "Nevada," he said. "It's always nice to see you."

"You son of a bitch…" I began.

"Shut up!" he thundered, his voice like a mountain tearing itself apart. It stopped me in my tracks instantly. I'd heard Dan shout plenty of times, but he'd never erupted at me like that before. "You sit the fuck down, and you shut the fuck up!" He pointed at the chair in front of his desk that Harry had been sitting in when I'd arrived.

Telling me what to do was, historically speaking, not such a great idea. But my energy was fading quickly and I'd lost my train of thought when he blew up at me. I tried to think of a cutting remark but drew a blank. Frustrated with myself, I sat down.

Dan stood up and I could see that he was shaking in rage. I'd crossed a line with him, a line I hadn't even known was there to cross. Maybe I should have started with "hello" before I cussed him out.

"Do you have any idea what you look like right now?" he asked.

"I took a shower…" I started.

"You look like *shit*!" he continued. "Absolute shit! You look like some goddamn thing the cat dragged in and then dragged back outside to die."

I stood up, trying to hide the fact that my legs were beginning to tremble. "I don't have to take this."

Dan took a step around his desk, fists clenched. "Sit in the fucking chair," he warned me.

Dan and I had gone at it before, plenty of times, but it had only ever been words. Things had never gotten physical between us. He just wasn't that kind of guy. But now I wasn't sure if he was willing to go there or not. If he wanted to take things to the next level I wasn't going to be able to put up much of a fight. On a better day, maybe. His size would be a problem, but I was faster, and I'd earned a black belt in Shotokan karate while I'd been a cop.

I sat back down. "This isn't going the way I had it planned," I noted.

Dan ignored my attempt at levity. "I am so fucking sick of you, Nevada," he continued. "I am sick of watching you kill yourself." He went back to his side of the desk. "You know what? Here." He opened his desk drawer and took out a .38 revolver. He turned the handle toward me and slammed it down on his desk. "Do it," he said, pointing at the gun. "Put that in your mouth and be done with this shit." He sat down in his chair and glared at me.

I stared back at him, stunned. I'd expected him to be angry with me, sure. But I'd never seen him like this before.

I'd have been lying if I said the gun didn't tempt me. Part of me wanted to pick it up and hold it, to feel the cool steel of the barrel, and to find out just what I'd do next.

If I'd been alone it might have been a different story, but I wasn't going to shoot myself in front of Dan. I might have deserved that, but he didn't.

"I'm sorry," I said, my hands clasped together on my lap.

"You *are* sorry," he said. Some of the anger had left his voice, but there was plenty left to spare. *And pain*, I thought. I'd hurt him badly.

We sat there in silence for a moment. I had no idea what to say to make any of this better. "Do you think maybe we could start this conversation over?" I asked. "Hi, Dan!" I said with mock cheerfulness. "How have you been?"

"No," he said, no longer looking at me. His eyes were wet. He wasn't crying, but this was as close as I'd ever seen him to it.

I sighed. "What do you want me to say?"

He looked back at me now. "I have been watching someone I love die," he said.

Was his mother ill? I started to ask him but then I realized he'd been talking about me.

"You have been dying for three years," he said. His voice carried a quiet urgency. "Maybe even longer than that. I won't even..." he waved a hand at me. "How much do you even weigh now?"

"Never ask a woman how much she weighs," I said. But the truth was I had no idea. Certainly a lot less than when I'd been healthy.

"You look like a damn skeleton."

On any other day a comment like that would have led to angry words being exchanged, but he'd managed to take the fight right out of me. "It's not that bad."

"It's exactly that bad."

"Well," I said.

"Well," he repeated.

We sat there for another minute but I didn't have any excuses left to make about my drinking or my health. He wasn't going to hear that today, and he was right. I knew I was full of shit.

I decided to try a different tack. "Why did you give Alan Davies my name?"

"You're a detective, aren't you? Why do you think, dumbass?"

I already knew the answer, didn't I? "You had some romantic notion that working a case could lead to my salvation," I said. "Especially if there was a child involved." I sighed. "You thought this might be just what I need to turn my life around before it's too late."

He nodded. "I would have phrased it differently," he said. "But yeah. That's about it."

"Yeah." I sighed again. "It's really not, Dan."

"We'll see. At least we'll have you doing something useful before your organs start failing. Have you seen a doctor recently?"

I stifled a laugh. "What do you think?"

He nodded. "Well, I can't force you to go to a rehab, and I know nobody will ever talk you into it. So there's this. The work."

I tried to think of something clever to say. Everything he

was saying was true, of course. I knew I was dying. I just didn't care. I hadn't cared in a long time.

"Did you guys really grow up together?" I asked.

"We knew each other. The kids in a neighborhood always know each other, you know? We weren't all that close but I thought he was a good guy, back then."

"And now he's the Godfather. He makes the deals people can't refuse."

The corner of his mouth twitched up. Good. I'd nearly made him laugh. I'd always been good at that. I was also secretly pleased that someone finally got one of my Mafia jokes.

"Something like that," Dan said. "I hadn't seen him in years, until he called me."

"You guys sound like a *Lifetime* movie." I deepened my voice to sound like I was narrating a movie trailer. "'They grew up together on the mean streets of El Cajon. Now one's a cop, and one's a criminal.'"

Dan shrugged. "If I ever get him on a murder, I'm not going to lose any sleep putting him away."

I nodded. Typical, incorruptible Dan. "What do you think about the case?"

"I think it's a domestic dispute."

"Then why get me involved?"

"Didn't we just have this conversation?"

"You probably could have found something else for me to do, if you really wanted to."

"Well, this is what landed on my desk," he said. "And maybe it's not a domestic thing. Even if it is, it gets you out of that house for a few days. It'll be a few days you're not drinking yourself to death."

I decided to let that one go. "You think there's any chance Davies is an abuser?"

"I wouldn't swear to it, but I doubt it. He never seemed like the type to me."

"He's a criminal."

"Doesn't mean he hits his wife or the kid. And he told me he'd consider the matter closed if you gave him your word that they were somewhere safe. Even if he changes his mind, he's not fool enough to threaten you."

"You think I intimidate him?"

"I don't know," Dan said. "But I know I do."

"Aw," I said, clasping my hands together under my chin. "My hero!"

"Shut up."

I took a breath. The hairs on the back of my neck were suddenly standing up. I had the feeling I'd missed something. "Does this seem strange to you?" I asked.

"What?"

"If your wife took your kid and left town, would you be satisfied as long as you knew that they were safe?"

"I don't have a wife or a kid."

"Stretch your big detective imagination," I said.

"I get the idea this kind of dispute is typical for them," Dan said. "So maybe he's used to it."

"Maybe," I said. "But the money…"

"What's he paying you?"

"Thirty thousand dollars."

Dan's eyes widened slightly. "*Thirty thousand?* You're serious?"

"Yeah. I don't know what the going rate on this kind of thing is, but that seems pretty excessive."

Dan opened his desk drawer and started looking through it. "I have his number in here somewhere. I'm calling him."

"No," I said, a little too quickly. Dan looked up in surprise. "I mean, it's his money to spend, and he can afford it. I'm sure it's a normal kind of expense for him." I was sure of nothing of the kind. The truth was I wanted Davies's money. Well, the real truth was that I *needed* the money. I didn't have the luxury to want it.

"All right," Dan said. "If you get the idea something's not right, call me. I'll put cops on it. Deal?"

"Deal."

He took the .38 off the desk and put it back in his desk drawer.

"What would you have done if I'd shot myself?" I asked.

"Do you really think I'd hand you a loaded gun?" He shrugged.

I laughed. Of course it hadn't been loaded. After a moment, Dan laughed, too.

"Look, the last time we spoke…" I began.

"Forget it."

"No. I was horrible to you. I'm sorry."

He looked at me for a moment. "All right."

"*All right?* That's it?"

"I really can't imagine what you went through," Dan said. "Maybe if I had I could have been a better friend to you and kept you from…" he looked at my sunken cheeks and shook his head. "From this."

"Nobody was going to keep me from this," I said quietly.

"Maybe. Maybe not."

We sat in silence for a moment, then Dan decided to take a poke at the elephant in the room. "Have you heard from him recently?"

"He sent a card on my last birthday."

He nodded. "You send it to the lab?"

"No. I just added it to the collection."

"Nevada," he began, his tone angry.

"You think the Laughing Man is going to leave fingerprints on a card? Or his DNA? Maybe he was nice enough to lick the envelope for us? Be serious."

Dan sighed. He knew I was right. "What did the card say?"

"It had two kittens on the front, one with his arm over the other's shoulder. Inside it said, 'Have a purrfect birthday.' See, they're mixing 'purr' and 'perfect,'" I explained.

"I got the humor," he said. "Did he write anything?"

I thought about lying to him, but what was the point of that at this stage? "He wrote, 'Miss you.' And he drew the face, of course." The Laughing Man always drew the face. That horrible, laughing face.

Dan's lips were pressed tightly together. I didn't need to ask what was going on in his head. Dan was a good cop. Honest. By the book. But if he ever caught up with the Laughing Man, there was never going to be a trial. The Laughing Man wouldn't live long enough to see the inside of a courthouse. Hell, he probably wouldn't live long enough to see the inside of a patrol car.

"All right," Dan said finally.

"I haven't been watching the news lately," I said, "but I take it he's still inactive? Seems like you'd have sent someone over otherwise."

Dan nodded. "He's been dark for three years. I don't know how he does it."

"How he does what?"

"How does he resist the urge?"

"It was never about compulsion." I shrugged. "It was just a game for him. That's all."

"You told me that once before," Dan said. "I didn't believe you then."

"There's your proof," I said. "He stopped killing because he lost his playmate. He lost *me*. Now he has nobody to…" I trailed off.

"Nobody to play with?"

"Yeah."

"There are other cops out there, you know."

"I was the only one he ever respected."

Dan snorted. "Sick freak."

"Him or me?"

Dan stared at me for a moment. "Maybe don't answer that," I said.

He took in a deep breath and let it out slowly. "So what are you going to do?"

"I don't know," I said. "Work the case, I guess. Go toss her condo. Look for clues."

"*Look for clues*? What are you now, Encyclopedia fucking Brown?"

"Give me a break," I said. "I don't know anything about working a missing persons case."

"Well, I'm sure you'll do fine. Have you eaten anything today?"

I hadn't touched any of the food at Davies's house, and to be honest, I didn't know how long my last blackout had lasted, or whether I had eaten anything while I'd been in it. Given my body's weakness, probably not. "I don't know," I admitted.

"Let me take you out, get you some soup," he offered.

"No."

"Nevada, you need to eat."

"I'll get something later," I lied.

"Promise me."

I hated making promises. Dan knew that. He also knew I

hated breaking them even more. But I didn't have any energy left to fight with him. "I'll eat today," I said. "I promise."

"Fine. Good luck finding your clues. Give us a call if you need some help."

I nearly laughed at that. "You really think anyone in this building actually wants to help me?"

"Yes," he said, looking me straight in the eyes. "I do."

I tried to think of a wiseass remark but came up with nothing. "Fine," I said. "I'll call if I need you."

"Promise me."

"Don't push your luck," I said. One promise in a day would have to be enough for now.

Chapter 5

Todd was still waiting for me outside police headquarters when I emerged from the building. He drove me home, muttering quietly to himself while he did so. I let him grumble. I no longer had the energy to do anything else. It had been a long day and I needed to rest soon. I was rarely conscious for more than a few hours at a time, and this morning's activity had all but wiped me out. Looking for clues was going to have to wait for a bit.

Back home I thought about telling poor Todd to wait for me again, but I decided I could drive myself around once I was ready to go. I had a few things I wanted to do at the house beforehand, though.

The briefcase Alan Davies had given me was stashed exactly where I'd left it. I opened it and dumped the contents out onto the bed. The ten thousand dollars turned out to be one stack of hundred-dollar bills bound together with a rubber band. There was no reason to have put it in a briefcase in the first place. A thick envelope would have worked just as well.

Maybe Davies just didn't like this briefcase and had wanted to get rid of it.

The bills themselves were in good condition, but they were definitely used and had none of the crispness you saw when someone opened a briefcase full of cash in a gangster movie. Actually seeing the money was remarkably anticlimactic. Everything looked better on film.

I thumbed through the stack of bills. Impressive looking or not, it was more money than I'd seen in a very long time. And I'd earned it just by listening to a guy talk and drinking his alcohol. It was nice work, if you could get it.

Then there was the matter of the twenty thousand dollars he wanted to pay me to find his family. I'd been right when I'd told Dan the money was excessive. If he hadn't wanted to hire a private investigator that was his prerogative, but he probably could have hired someone to do this job for a few hundred dollars. I'd have done it for a few thousand, to be honest. I'd been gouging him earlier more to amuse myself than anything else. And judging from the speed with which he acquiesced, I probably could have taken him for a lot more.

What wasn't Davies telling me? He had to be holding something back. I still wondered whether he could be abusing his family. If he was, he'd chosen the wrong person to send to find them. There wasn't any amount of money that would make me give up his wife's location if she asked me not to. I'd just call Dan and he'd send an army of police officers to Davies's estate to tear the place apart. Or maybe I'd leave the police out of it and pay Davies a visit myself. It would probably depend a lot on how much I'd had to drink at the time.

I went into the kitchen and poured an inch of vodka into a tumbler. If I didn't do a certain amount of maintenance, withdrawal was sure to hit me hard. I didn't know if I was so far gone that *delirium tremens* would take hold and I'd start having hallucinations and seizures, and I had no interest in finding out.

It was time to do something about the smell in my living room. I took a large Hefty bag out of a kitchen cabinet and spent twenty minutes picking up old bottles and moldy garbage. When the bag was full I took it outside to the dumpster. I opened two of the living room windows to let fresh air in. I didn't have any kind of air freshener, but I could pick up a can of something when I went out. Maybe I could make the place smell like a person actually lived here.

When the cleaning was done I poured myself another inch of vodka and took it into my bedroom. I needed to lay down. I'd promised Dan I would eat today, and I would. I'd go out and get some food soon. But first I needed a little nap. Then I'd eat, and get to work, but first…

The sun was going down when I woke up. I lay on my bed for a moment, torn between the need to use the bathroom and the desire not to move. In the end, the bathroom won out. When I was done I washed my hands and cupped some cold water into my mouth. How long had it been since I'd actually drank any water? I couldn't remember. I'd nearly forgotten what it tasted like.

The reflection in my mirror didn't look like the me I remembered. Dan had said I looked like a skeleton and he wasn't all that far off. My cheeks were hollow and I'd lost a ton of weight, but the most troublesome thing was my eyes. They had a lifeless glaze I'd seen before, but only at crime scenes. In the eyes of the dead.

How long could I live like this, realistically? Six months? Nine? Another year didn't seem all that likely.

I made a halfhearted attempt to brush my hair. After thirty seconds I found that I didn't care enough to keep at it. I looked marginally better, but I could probably still be mistaken for a homeless person if I went for a walk downtown.

My vodka glass was still in the bedroom where I'd left it. I was disappointed to see that it was empty, but I decided not to fill it right away. I had some things I needed to do before I knocked myself out again.

There was a 7-11 at the intersection about a block away from my house. I walked there slowly, trying to push past the weakness in my legs. Inside I picked up a box of instant noodle soup and two cans of V-8. I needed calories if I was going to be able to function, and this would be a good start.

When I got back to my house I put water on to boil and drank half a can of V-8. That would get some vitamins in me, at least, and it was easier than trying to make a salad. When the water was ready I tore open a pouch of the soup and dumped it into a coffee mug, then added the hot water. It smelled strangely appealing, certainly more than any soup that came out of a pouch had a right to.

I sipped the hot soup slowly as I went into the dining room. I had to clear more garbage off the table to make a spot for the file Chandler Emerson had given me earlier. It would take several more Hefty bags to make the rest of the house livable, but the living room had been enough of a start for now. Everything else could wait. For now I needed to read.

As I'd suspected earlier, there wasn't all that much in the file. The first page had a photocopy of Heather Davies's driver's license. She was 34 years old, had blue eyes, blonde hair, and weighed 128 pounds. That eliminated maybe half the female population of San Diego, leaving me the other half to wade through. I wasn't going to find Heather by driving up and down the streets and looking for her.

The rest of the paperwork was background information. Heather had worked as a dancer at a place called Pogo's, which I assumed was a strip club. I'd never heard of it. She and Davies had been married twelve years ago. They'd been legally separated for a year with joint custody of their daughter, but there was no divorce paperwork in the file. Maybe they really were trying to work things out. Or maybe Davies just hadn't included that part.

A family tree that looked like it had been printed off of a website was included among the papers. Several of the names, including those of her parents, were marked as "deceased." Others had addresses and phone numbers attached, but none lived in California. The closest family she had was an uncle in Utah. Somehow I doubted that was where she'd gone.

Heather's current address was in La Jolla, an upscale enclave just north of San Diego. I was surprised to see that the condo itself was leased by a company called "A. N. Davies Holdings," and Chandler Emerson's name was on the paperwork as an officer of that company. Her husband was paying for the condo, then. I wondered if that were part of the separation agreement.

Emerson had taped a key to Heather's condo to the inside cover of the file. At least, I assumed it was her condo. I supposed it could be a key to *his* house and he'd been making a very ambitious pass at me, but that seemed unlikely.

All together, there was very little in the file I could use other than Heather's current address. Was this what passed for a dossier these days? It seemed like James Bond always got more to work with.

Or had the paperwork been presented this way because that was where Davies wanted me to start? Was he manipulating me?

How did cops usually work missing persons cases? I'd really only seen them on television, and I didn't have a sassy partner to banter with until some plot contrivance came along and broke the case open for us. Taking a look at Heather's condo seemed like a reasonable place to start, though. For all I knew Heather and Anna were both up there and this was all a huge misunderstanding.

My hands were starting to tremble. It was time for a little maintenance. I went back into the kitchen and didn't bother with a glass this time. I took one good swallow out of the nearest open vodka bottle, then chased it with the other half of the V-8. That should be enough to keep the shakes at bay for a while, but not enough that I was going to need a nap.

I found a large envelope and counted out $5000 of the cash Davies had given me into it. The rest of the money I tucked under my mattress. It wasn't the world's best hiding place, but it would do for now.

My house had a garage attached with a connecting door in the hallway next to the laundry room. I had an old Mustang Cobra parked inside, and a Kawasaki Ninja next to it. I hadn't been on the motorcycle in years. Balance was a critical part of riding a bike, and I didn't have much balance to speak of anymore. Maybe if I managed to stay sober for a few days I could get the bike cleaned up and take it out. It would need some work first. The battery was probably dead and I was sure it could use an oil change and fresh fluids, but that wouldn't take me long to do. But what were the odds I'd ever be sober long enough to do any of that? Not very good.

I started the Mustang and put the envelope full of cash on the passenger seat next to the Davies file. As my garage door rolled up I held my hands out in front of me and watched them for a moment. They were far from steady, but they weren't shaking. I should be able to pass as a normal person for a few hours, at least.

When the garage door was open I pulled out and then waited as it rolled shut. The Mustang's controls felt unfamiliar to me, a little like being behind the wheel of a new car for the first time. It had been a while since I'd driven. Most of the things I needed from day to day were located within easy walking distance. Well, the walking was less easy than it used to be. These days I needed to rest after I'd gone two blocks. Three felt like a marathon.

Heather's condo in La Jolla was arguably closer than my landlord's place in La Mesa, but I didn't want to leave the car with $5000 in cash sitting in it, envelope or no. It took me about ten minutes to navigate Ocean Beach's narrow streets until I reached I-10, and then I was headed east on the freeway.

Rush hour was winding down but there was still plenty of traffic heading towards the bedroom communities east of San Diego. I set the cruise control for two miles per hour under the speed limit and concentrated on keeping the car centered in my lane. I wasn't drunk by a long shot, but I probably wouldn't pass a breathalyzer test if I got pulled over. Any CHP officer that recognized me probably wouldn't ticket me for a DUI, but odds were Dan Evans wouldn't be thrilled when his home phone rang and he was asked if he could send someone out to pick up his former detective.

La Mesa was about twenty minutes away. I hadn't seen the Harrisons in a few years. Usually I just mailed them a check for the rent, but I wasn't about to go deposit ten thousand dollars in cash in the bank. That was what drug dealers did. Stupid drug dealers, anyway. Handing that much cash to a bank teller was like saying, "I'd really like the IRS to come visit me at my house." And ever since 9/11, the FBI might come along with them just to check and see if you were hiding any of bin Laden's relatives in your closet.

The Harrisons lived on a quiet cul-de-sac on the eastern end of the city. I knew the address by heart but it still took me a few minutes to find their house nestled among the perfectly manicured palm trees that lined the streets here. Most of the people who lived in this neighborhood were retired and fairly well-to-do financially. The place had a "Mayberry" vibe I didn't much care for, except for the fact that it was quiet. I was a big fan of quiet these days.

I rang their doorbell just after 7:30, which I figured was late enough that I wouldn't be interrupting their dinner. A moment passed and I could hear voices and people moving from within, and then the door opened and I saw Roger Harrison. He looked a great deal older than the last time I'd seen him. It had been several years, admittedly, but I was still taken aback by the change. Time really flew when you weren't having fun.

Roger looked as startled to see me as I felt to see him. "Nevada," he said softly.

"Mr. Harrison."

"Roger," he corrected me, opening the door wider.

"Who is it?" a woman's voice called from behind him. Mary Harrison stepped into view and nearly dropped the glass of water she was carrying. "Nevada James!"

"Yeah," I said. "Hi." I was hoping to make this quick. I held up the envelope of cash. "I owe you guys…"

"Come in! Come in!" Mary called, beckoning me. Roger stepped aside to make a path for me.

"I really can't," I said.

"Nonsense!" Mary said. "Roger, go put the kettle on."

I held up the envelope again. "I just came to pay rent," I insisted. "I owe you guys a lot and I'm sorry I didn't take care of it sooner." I handed the envelope to Roger, who took it a bit hesitantly. "That will cover what I owe you and more."

Mary Harrison took a step closer and looked at my face. "You've been sick," she said disapprovingly. "And my word, you've gotten so skinny!"

"Yeah," I said. "I have been sick." I was starting to sweat in the cool night air. Goddamn withdrawal. I hadn't had enough to drink before I got in my car.

Boy, did that sound strange in my head.

"Come in, Nevada," Mary said soothingly. "I'll fix you something to eat."

I had to admit that sounded good, but the last thing I wanted to do was sit with them and come up with believable lies to explain what I'd been doing for the last three years.

They didn't know the things that hadn't been in the papers. "I can't," I said. "I'm…I'm working a case."

Mary's eyes widened. "You're working again?" Roger beamed at me and I was immediately embarrassed. This was like being a toddler and having your grandparents congratulate you for using the toilet instead of crapping your pants. You're not *supposed* to crap your pants.

"Not officially," I said. "I'm not a cop anymore, but I'm helping…someone…with something." What was I supposed to tell them? I was doing errands for a mob boss?

"Good for you!" Roger couldn't contain his enthusiasm.

"Yeah, it is," I said. "It's getting me out of the house, you know? It's good to be doing something."

"You were so good as a police officer," Mary said, and now there were tears in her eyes. "It's your calling."

I shook my head. "I'm not so sure about that."

"I am."

"Anyway, I have to get working on this case," I said. "So, I just wanted to give you that rent and say sorry it's late."

"Come see us soon," Mary said. "We do worry about you."

"We do," Roger agreed.

"And for goodness sake, eat something," Mary admonished me. "You don't want to look like one of those skinny models."

"I'll work on it," I said.

"Wait a minute, I'll fix you a sandwich."

"I've got plenty of food at home," I lied, taking a step back. I felt my legs starting to tremble. "I've really got to get going."

"Take care," Roger said.

"Come see us," Mary repeated.

"I will," I said. "I promise." The words got out before I remembered how much I hated making promises. Now I was going to have to come see them. Well, I hadn't said *when*.

I got in my car and drove a block before pulling over again. I needed to pull myself together and I didn't want the Harrisons to look out of their window and see me sitting in my car while I was doing it. My sweating seemed to be slowing down now that I was sitting again. I still felt weak but that was par for the course these days. I'd probably feel this way until I'd eaten solid food for a few days in a row and gotten my metabolism going again.

I shut my eyes. How stupid was I? I'd meant to ask them about their son, but I'd been in such a hurry to get out of there I'd completely forgotten about it. I'd been avoiding human contact for so long I'd forgotten how to talk to people like a normal person.

My hands were less steady than they had been earlier, but they still weren't shaking. I could keep going for a while yet. I needed to stay sober for a few more hours, at least long enough to get up to Heather's condo and take a look around.

I took a deep breath. There. I was okay. Things were going to be fine. I put the car in gear and pulled away from the curb. Next stop: La Jolla.

Chapter 6

It took me a good half hour on the freeways to reach the exit that led into La Jolla, and then another half hour of searching to find Heather's condo. That would teach me not to look at a map first.

Heather lived in a luxury two-building complex on a ridge overlooking the Pacific Ocean. I could only imagine what a place like this cost. The ten grand Davies had given me earlier might be enough to cover one lease payment. Then again, it might well not.

Heather's complex had a small guest parking lot adjacent to the resident parking. That was something I didn't see very often. In my part of the city an apartment building might have one guest parking space near the building management office. Two would be a luxury. An entire lot was just extravagant.

I locked the car up and headed into the lobby, which seemed to be constructed entirely out of glass. People always tell you not to go outside during an earthquake, but if the ground started shaking when I was in here, I'd be running for the door like a teenager going to see a boy band.

A security guard in a dark suit sat by himself at a desk in the lobby. He looked up at me and smiled as I entered. "Good evening, Ms. James," he said.

I blinked in surprise. "If that was a guess, it was pretty amazing," I told him.

"Mr. Emerson called ahead and told me you would be stopping by. He was good enough to describe you."

I nearly asked *how* Emerson had described me, but I wasn't sure I wanted to hear it. I wasn't sure how the guard even knew who Emerson was, but then I remembered the lawyer's name had been on the lease paperwork. The staff here must be used to dealing with him.

Not having to explain who I was and what I was doing here only made things easier for me. "You have any problem with me going up to her place and taking a look around?"

"Not at all," the guard said. "If you didn't bring your key I can let you in."

I held up the key Emerson had given me. "You guys think of everything."

"That's what we get paid for," he said.

I hit the button for the elevator and the doors slid open instantly. So far this visit was going really well.

Heather Davies's condo was on the third floor, on the side of the building that faced the ocean. I knocked at the door, not really expecting a response, but it seemed like the polite thing to do. For all I knew she really was just hiding out here, not wanting to be bothered.

There was no response. I knocked a second time and put my ear up to the door to listen. I couldn't hear anything coming from inside. I stepped back and looked up and down the hallway, half-expecting curious neighbors to be peeking out their doors at me. Nobody was. The whole place was as silent as a tomb. Quiet was probably one of the luxuries these people paid for.

I put the key in the lock and turned it. The door opened easily, and my hand instinctively reached for the waist holster where I used to keep my gun. Of course I wasn't armed. Old habits. But I had alarm bells going off in my head. Something was wrong inside the condo.

The lights were on.

"Hello?" I called. There was no response. I pushed the door open the rest of the way. "Hello?" I was louder this time, but there was still nothing. I could hear music playing softly. It was coming from another room. I recognized the melody, but couldn't place it. It was from a movie I'd seen, but I couldn't think of which one.

I stepped into the condo and closed the door slowly behind me. "Hello?" I called a third time. If anybody was in here, they had to be aware of my presence by now. I was making enough racket that I'd have been surprised if the neighbors couldn't hear me, thick walls or not. Could Heather and Anna be hiding in here? If so, why?

Heather's condo was furnished much as I might have expected any upscale condo in this area to be. She had considerably better taste than her husband. There wasn't a single marble column in sight, and nothing a person would call ostentatious. She had money, or at least access to money, but she spent it well.

I headed down the hall towards the source of the music. It was so familiar. Where had I heard it before?

The music was coming from a bedroom I assumed belonged to Anna. Unless it was her mother who had decorated her walls with posters of Justin Bieber, but that seemed unlikely. A large flat-screen television was set up in a media center against one wall. It was on, and looping the DVD menu from one of the Harry Potter movies. So that was where the music was coming from. Every time the menu reset itself the music started up from the beginning again. So someone had been about to watch a movie, or someone had been watching a movie when they'd been interrupted. The movie would have played through to the end and then returned to the menu, where it had been stuck in an endless loop ever since. There was no way to tell how long this had been going on. Barring a power outage, I didn't see a reason why it would ever stop.

I looked around the bedroom for anything suspicious, but nothing in the room seemed out of place until I turned back to the door. There was a small black scuff mark about three feet up on the door frame. I knelt down to take a closer look. I was no forensic scientist, but it looked like a mark made by a shoe. There was the tiniest bit of tread from a sneaker visible. Ten-year-old girls didn't typically kick walls, as far as I remembered. I hadn't. But one who was being carried out of a room against her will might.

I shut off the television to get rid of the noise, then stood absolutely still for a moment and just listened. I couldn't hear a sound. Either someone was playing the best game of hide-and-seek ever, or there was nobody here.

The guest bathroom was just down the hall. Nothing in there seemed out of place. The most interesting thing in the medicine cabinet was a bottle of Advil, and when I twisted it open I wasn't surprised to find that it did indeed contain Advil.

Back in the hallway, I pulled open the door to a hall closet. It contained a vacuum cleaner, a broom, and other cleaning supplies. Nothing unusual in there.

Heather Davies had the master bedroom, the centerpiece of which was a queen size bed. It had been neatly made sometime before and the room was tastefully decorated. No Justin Bieber posters in here. I opened her closet and found it full of carefully hung clothes. There were no gaps among them to suggest that she'd taken anything out to pack for a trip. The shoe rack below told the same story. It was lined with a variety of shoes from one end to the other, with a gap on one side that would have accommodated exactly one pair of shoes. If she had planned to go away with her daughter, even for just a few days, I was sure she'd have taken some of this stuff. Even I took more than one pair of shoes on a short trip, and I was the least girly girl anyone had ever met.

My hand clutched the air where my handle of my gun would have been again, only to drop back to my side. Something was very wrong here.

I went back to the living room to look around. This time I noticed that the carpet near the door had been vacuumed recently, but *only* the carpet near the door. That was odd. Looking closer, I could see that there were a number of track marks still in the carpet. I knelt down to get a better look. Some of the tracks had definitely been left by a vacuum, but there were other marks that were too wide and deep to have been made by someone cleaning. Something with wheels had been here recently, and it would have been something large and heavy. I traced one of the marks with my finger. Luggage? No, the marks were too deep, and they were in the wrong pattern. Two large objects had been here, each having four wheels on a wide rectangular frame. They'd been wheeled in, stopped, and then wheeled back out.

I couldn't think of anything that made marks like the ones I was seeing, unless someone had wheeled two upright pianos in here and then decided to get rid of them.

The kitchen was on the other end of the living room, to the right of the entry door. An enormous refrigerator was full of diet soda and other things to drink. I opened one and drank half of it. Looking for clues was thirsty work.

The refrigerator had two crisper drawers. I opened one and took out a head of lettuce. The leaves were black around the edges. There was a bag of carrots that hadn't been opened yet. I tore a hole in it and pulled out a carrot, unsurprised to find it limp. All of the fresh vegetables were in different stages of decomposition, all well beyond edible. They'd been in here untouched for quite a while.

A line of cabinets was set in the walls above the kitchen counters. I opened them one by one, revealing plates, bowls, glasses, and finally the liquor I'd been hoping to find. There was no vodka but Heather had a bottle of good tequila that was well outside my normal price range. I took it down and twisted it open. The smell hit my nostrils with the effect that steak might have had on a starving man. I took a long sniff, then treated myself to a small sip directly from the bottle.

It was amazing stuff. The tequila went down my throat with a warmth that felt like visiting distant relatives on Christmas. I took a deep breath, then chased the liquor with a swallow of diet soda. That was better.

I took the bottle back into the living room and looked around again. There had to be more to this story. What was I missing? And what was *that*? I could see what looked like a dark green scratch on the wall a few feet away from the door, but it was just above my head. That hadn't been anybody's shoe, unless it had a green sole and had been thrown with considerable force. I reached up and ran my fingers across the mark. Something had definitely hit the wall here, but what could it have been?

A set of shelves near the television caught my eye. It held an assortment of ceramic animals painted in different colors. I saw an elephant, a camel, a family of little dogs, and another family of cats. The figures didn't appear to be part of a single set; Heather must have been collecting these for years. But there was a large space empty between a rainbow-painted gecko and a long-necked giraffe. Something else had been on this shelf.

I didn't see a trash can in the living room, but there had been one in the kitchen. I went back there and looked inside the trash can, unsurprised to find several green ceramic shards at the bottom of the bag. I picked them out one by one and laid them out on the counter. It didn't take long to put them back into an approximation of their rightful places. This had been a turtle about the size of a softball, before the figurine had met its unfortunate end.

I took one of the shards into the living room and held it up against the scratch on the wall. The colors matched. Someone, most likely Heather Davies, had hurled the turtle at the wall hard enough to shatter it. The ceramic was heavy; it wouldn't have broken easily. It didn't seem likely that Heather had been angry with the turtle. A more reasonable theory was that she had been meaning to do some damage to someone standing near the door.

Returning to the kitchen, I took another swallow of the tequila, but this time my stomach rebelled and I vomited it up into the sink almost instantly. It took a moment of clutching the side of the counter and breathing hard to get myself back under control. When I had my breath, I took another drink, swallowing hard and fighting off the nausea that followed to keep it down. When the nausea passed, I took another drink for good measure. I didn't have time for withdrawal symptoms tonight. If I didn't keep drinking I was going to be useless before long.

I wiped my mouth with my sleeve and then put the turtle back together. Heather could get some superglue when she came back and fix the little guy herself. *If* she came back.

I took another lap around the apartment but couldn't think of anything else to do here. This was looking very much like an abduction to me. I couldn't think of anything else that made sense.

The security guard I'd talked to before was still in the lobby when I went back downstairs. "Everything all right?" he asked me.

At first I thought he was asking if *I* was all right. My eyes were probably bloodshot from vomiting, and I knew I couldn't smell all that great. But then I guessed he was talking about my search of Heather's condo. "When did you see Heather Davies last?" I asked.

"A week ago, maybe." He frowned. "I'm not sure, to be

honest."

"She got a delivery recently," I said. "Do you know what that was about?"

The guard took a clipboard out of his desk and began flipping through the sheets on it. "Here it is," he said. "Furniture delivery the Tuesday before last."

I wasn't sure if that had been ten days ago or not, but it would have been close. "Delivery from where?"

"It doesn't say," he said. "Just that they were in at 2:53 pm, out at 3:20. Two crates in and out."

Crates. That made sense. It would be hard to drag a woman and a child out of a security building like this. But if you knocked them out or drugged them and then shut them up in wooden crates, nobody would think to look twice at you as you wheeled them outside. "Would anyone here have looked inside the crates?" I asked.

He shook his head. "Oh, no. We take security pretty seriously, but we'd never inspect anyone's property like that. We're not really expecting to be bombed," he laughed.

"All right," I said. "Thanks for your help."

I left the building behind and went back to my car. This wasn't at all how I'd expected this visit to go. I'd gone in thinking I might find some clues as to where Heather Davies had taken off to. A copy of a hotel reservation printout. A Lonely Planet guide to somewhere warm and sunny. Instead I was nearly certain that Heather Davies and her daughter had been violently abducted from their condo. Those crates for the "furniture delivery" had been empty when they'd arrived at the building, and full when they'd left. I had no idea whether the women were dead or alive when they'd left the building. There was no blood visible in the condo, but blood could be cleaned, and any smell left lingering from the chemicals the kidnappers might have used would have long since dissipated by now.

I sat in my car and thought about it. Did Alan Davies know about the abduction? Was that why he was paying me such an absurd amount of money to find his family? Or had he been honest with me when I'd been at his estate? I didn't have enough evidence to go either way yet, and I hadn't brought the card with his phone number on it along with me. I couldn't have called him, anyway. I had no idea what I'd done with my cell phone; I couldn't even remember the last time I'd seen it.

It could wait. I'd be in touch with Davies soon, and if I found out he'd lied to me…well, I wasn't the type to pout and stomp my feet.

Chapter 7

I drove home, enjoying the warm feeling Heather's tequila had left in my stomach. It occurred to me that I'd be able to afford good liquor once I'd finished this job. I'd been drinking store-brand rotgut for so long I'd forgotten what the good stuff tasted like. It didn't matter much in the end. Alcohol had the same effect whether you were paying four dollars per bottle or four hundred, but if you were going to kill yourself drinking, you might as well do it with some style.

Once I was back home I decided I didn't feel like navigating the Mustang into my cluttered garage, so I parked at the curb instead. I'd need the car in the morning, anyway. Or in the afternoon. Whenever I woke up.

Maybe I'd drive up to Solana Beach and confront Davies with what I'd found. It was hard to read people on the phone, but if he were lying to me in person, I was pretty sure I'd be able to tell. In the old days I'd been a walking lie detector. I knew my senses were nowhere near as finely tuned as they'd been when I was on the police force, but I was willing to bet they'd still be good for something.

As I was heading up the path toward my front door I noticed a black Lincoln pulling in to park behind my car. One of Davies's people? Had Emerson come to get an update? The timing was uncanny, unless he had been waiting here for me. But in that case, why hadn't he been parked in front of the house when I'd arrived?

I started to unlock my front door, but fumbled with the keys and dropped them. As I knelt down I saw Todd getting out of the driver's side of the car. He was out of his chauffeur's uniform, having changed into jeans and a black leather jacket. Had he come to take me up to see Davies? There was no way in hell I was doing that tonight. The only thing I was interested in right now was sleep.

Todd had a determined look on his face as he started up the path toward me, his hands tucked in his pockets. What was that about?

I turned the key in the door's lock and pushed the door open half an inch. Then I looked back at my visitor. "Todd, I really don't have time for…"

Todd took his hands out of his pockets. In his right hand he held a small automatic pistol. He raised it toward me and pulled the trigger, putting a bullet into the door just behind my head.

The noise from the shot cut off all the sound around me and left a ringing in my ears. Startled, I turned and looked at the hole Todd had just put in my door. A tiny curl of smoke rose from the wood where the bullet had gone in. What the hell was Todd thinking about? Was he actually trying to *kill* me?

Seriously?

I looked back at Todd. His eyes were wide with fear, but I could see his finger tightening on the trigger again. His second shot went wide, farther off target than the first.

And then the adrenaline hit me like a bolt of lightning. I turned and kicked my door open the rest of the way, then dove inside the house as Todd's third shot went over my head, close enough that I could hear the little *pop* as it passed by my ear. I landed hard on the carpet and spun around to kick the door shut. That would buy me about two seconds, if I was lucky. I scrambled to my feet and ran for the kitchen. I had knives in the kitchen. Knives would be good right now.

The door burst open behind me and Todd fired twice more, neither shot coming close to me. I was willing to bet this was the first time he had tried to kill someone. If he'd had even a little more experience, or been a little more sure of himself, he could have made easy work of me outside. If he'd taken three steps closer before drawing his gun it would have been over before I'd have had time to react. But now Todd's own adrenaline surge was making his hands shake, sending his shots in every direction but their intended target.

He fired again and a bullet whizzed past, tearing a hole in the arm of my jacket but not piercing my skin. At least, I didn't think it had. As pumped up as I was, I doubted I'd be able to feel pain. But Todd's aim was getting better. I was never going to make it to the kitchen before he hit me.

I turned in mid-stride and tried to put the couch between me and Todd, thinking I might be able to make it into my bedroom and lock the door. That wouldn't hold him for long, but my bedroom had a large window. If I broke it open I could probably be through it and halfway down the block before he got to me.

It might have worked, but my foot slipped on a hamburger wrapper I'd somehow missed on my cleaning jag earlier and I fell to the ground. Todd fired two more shots, then his gun clicked on empty.

I got to my feet. Todd was staring at his gun in surprise, as if he couldn't believe he had run out of bullets. Did he think this was a videogame? "Dumbass," I said. My ears were still ringing but I could hear my own voice clearly enough, along with Todd's panting.

Todd looked up and then he actually threw the gun at me. I dodged it easily. "You suck at this," I sneered at him. Adrenaline and booze were doing a number on my emotions. I was enjoying this now. Death, my old friend, had taken another run at me. Death had missed.

Fighting Todd was pretty far down on the list of things I wanted to be doing right now, but he put his fists up and took a step toward me. He had a boxer's stance but looked untrained, as if he was trying to mimic something he had seen on television and not learned in a gym. He'd probably relied on his size to save him in fights before. He'd be used to intimidating people, and ending things with one good punch if a confrontation ever went that far. But the only chance he'd have ever had against me would have been to grapple. He could have wrapped me up and choked me out in a matter of seconds, if he'd had any idea how to actually use that size advantage of his. But the fool wanted to punch. Big mistake.

I put my left foot forward and set myself in a middle-height stance, weight on my back foot. If he wanted to fight I'd show him what Shotokan karate was about. But I wasn't going to make the first move. He would have to come at me and show me what he had.

Todd launched a slow but powerful punch at my head. It might have killed me if it had connected, but dodging it was child's play. He tried again but I danced out of the way. I could hear a police siren in the distance now. For the first time in my life I was glad that I had neighbors nearby. I'd never complain about their loud music again.

"You're out of time, big boy," I said. "Give it up."

Todd's attention wandered and I could have ended it right there by taking out one of his knees, but I wanted him talking, not screaming. I had questions for him, and once the police dragged him away I'd never have the chance to ask them.

"Is this because of the affair?" I asked. "Were you afraid I'd tell Davies about it?"

Todd glared at me, trying to look fierce, but I saw the desperation he was trying to hide and nearly felt sorry for him. Nearly. "Not you," he said. "I'm sorry. *He* said I have to kill you, or *he'll* tell." Todd still hadn't put his hands down. How did he think this was going to end?

"Who is going to tell?" I asked. "Tell me who sent you and this is over. Things are going to look a lot better for you if you surrender."

"I can't…"

"Nobody is hurt yet, Todd. You shot a gun off a couple times. That's all. If we work this right maybe you won't even get attempted murder for it."

Todd hesitated for just a moment, then he lunged at me. I

sidestepped and drove the forward edge of my hand into his throat, intending to end the fight in one shot. It was hard to punch someone when you couldn't breathe. But I heard Todd's windpipe crunch as I connected with his neck. He clutched at his throat with both hands and dropped to his knees with a thud.

"Shit," I said. I'd gone too far. Todd stared up at me, terror in his eyes. His fingers clawed at his throat as if he were trying to put the broken pieces in there back together. That was never going to happen. If he was lucky he had about a minute before he suffocated.

The police were getting closer, and an ambulance wouldn't be far behind them, but they would be far too late to help Todd.

I needed to think fast. What about a tracheotomy? I'd never been trained to do one, but I'd seen it on television and it looked like something I could manage. Or was that just the tequila talking? Probably, but what did I have to lose? What did I need? A knife? I ran into the kitchen to look for one, settling on a paring knife with a sharp point and thin blade. That would work. But he'd need something to breathe through once I'd made the hole in his throat. Some kind of tube. What about a straw? I had plenty of fast food crap lying around the house. A person could breathe through a straw if they tried, right? At least for a little while?

Todd was lying face-down on the floor when I went back into the living room with my knife and straw. I took a good look at him, but it was over. Todd didn't me to play amateur surgeon anymore. He was dead.

I went over to his body and looked down at him, still

holding my makeshift tools. Poor, stupid man. It would have been so simple to kill me.

I nudged his body with my foot. "How did you fuck that up?" I asked him quietly.

Todd was long past answering. Obviously the poor man hadn't been a killer. But I was. Todd was only my latest victim.

I went back into the kitchen and returned the knife to its drawer. Then I cracked open a new bottle of vodka. I took it into the living room and sat down on my couch, waiting for the police to come.

Chapter 8

Half an hour later a crime scene photographer was taking photos of Todd's corpse where he had fallen on my living room floor. Another investigator was prying a bullet out of my wall. Two homicide detectives I didn't know were standing in the corner, talking quietly between themselves. Earlier one of them had asked me if I minded if they made a pot of coffee. I told them I didn't have any coffee. One of the uniforms brought them some in paper cups from the 7-11 down the street.

The boys in blue had stormed my front door a few minutes after Todd's death. I'd been in the middle of a long drink from my bottle and held up a finger for them to wait. The uniforms recognized me instantly, of course. They'd locked the house down and, after making sure I didn't need medical attention, gone outside to wait for the detectives.

Sarah Winters had arrived a few minutes later. She'd brought along a blanket the EMTs outside had given her and had been trying to keep it draped over my shoulders. I shrugged it off every few minutes. I wasn't cold. I was numb. They didn't make a blanket for that.

I'd told Sarah most of the story, starting from when I'd first seen Todd outside my house. At first she'd taken notes down on a little pad, but after a few minutes she put the pad down on the table and just listened to me.

"That was lucky," she said, when I told her how I'd dropped Todd.

"No," I said. "It was an error in judgment. I didn't want to kill him."

"He'd have killed you."

I scoffed. "He'd have been doing me a fucking favor."

There was an engine noise from outside like someone had mistaken my street for a NASCAR track, and then I heard car tires screeching to a stop. It was followed by a ruckus at the door as a familiar voice shouted at the uniforms standing watch outside to get the hell out of his way. I sighed. This had been inevitable.

Dan Evans barreled into my house like a wrecking ball, his eyes wild. Sarah stood up to greet him. "Captain, I was..." she began.

"What in the *holy flying fuck*?" Dan interrupted.

"Captain..." Sarah tried again.

"No!" he snapped, stabbing a finger at her. He came over to where I was sitting and looked down at me. "Get up!"

I stood, not really wanting to make eye contact with him. "Hi, boss." I'd been trying to sound cheerful to lighten the mood a bit, but it ended up sounding kind of pathetic.

Dan put his hands on my shoulders and began patting me down. At first I thought he was checking me for weapons, but I quickly realized he was trying to see if I was hiding an injury. It was the kind of thing he'd expect from me. "I'm not hurt," I said gently.

"Shut up," he said. He knelt down on the carpet and ran his hands down each of my legs.

"He never hit me," I said. "Ruined a jacket, though." Todd's closest shot had punched a nice in-and-out hole in the arm of my jacket, but the bullet hadn't even grazed my skin. I wasn't sure where it had wound up. The CSI guys would find it eventually.

Dan stood up again. He glared at me for a moment, then I saw his face crack. He put his arms around me and hugged me tight.

I had been expecting him to chew me out. This was...not that. I put one arm around him and patted him gently on the back. "It's okay," I said. "I'm okay."

He pulled back. "This is really fucking far from okay," he said. He took a deep breath, then went over to look at Todd's body. One of the Medical Examiner's guys was bringing in a gurney. In a minute they'd hoist Todd onto it and take him away.

Dan put his hands on his hips. "Who the fuck is this guy?" he asked.

Sarah started to talk but Dan waved her off. "From her," he said, pointing at me.

"One of Davies's drivers," I told him.

Dan grunted and knelt down to get a better look at the

body. "Name."

"Todd something." Dan gave me a dark look. "I don't know his last name!" I protested.

Dan took a moment to examine Todd's body, then he stood up. "Why did he come after you?"

The best lies are mostly made up of the truth. You just change some of the details. "He had an affair with Heather Davies," I said. "I caught him on it this morning when he was driving me around. I think he was afraid I'd rat him out to his boss, so he came over to make sure I couldn't."

"Did he say anything to you?"

"He told me he was afraid Davies would kill him if he ever found out, when I talked to him before. I told him I'd keep the affair quiet, but I guess he didn't think he could take the chance."

Dan grunted and looked around the house, then motioned Sarah and the two other homicide detectives into a corner. I took a seat on the couch and watched as Sarah took the lead and described the progress of the attempted hit to the others. The bullet hole in the door. The others in the walls, which had been marked with tape by the CSI team. The confrontation behind the couch. She even pantomimed my striking Todd in the throat, actually coming close to the way I'd done it, although Sarah had no martial arts training and her "karate chop" looked comical to my eye.

She had all of it right, except I hadn't told her that Todd had been acting on someone else's orders. Or that I was sure Heather Davies and her daughter had been abducted from their condo. That would have been the smart thing to do, of course. But if I did, Dan would throw me over his shoulder and carry me straight to a safe house, and the SDPD would take over my case.

My case? I was a little surprised at myself. I hadn't thought of myself as having a case in a long time, but here I was getting territorial over it. Old habits.

I watched as two men heaved Todd's body onto the gurney and then rolled him out of my house. I had an almost overwhelming need to apologize to him, or to someone, but I held it in. I could not let the people in this house see me being weak.

My bottle sat on the table in front of me. I didn't touch it, as much as I wanted to. I wouldn't drink in front of Dan and Sarah. There would be time for that later.

Dan still had his hands on his hips, but he seemed satisfied by Sarah's explanation of events. The two nameless homicide detectives left the house and he and Sarah came back to where I was sitting on the couch. "CSI is going to finish up and then they'll get out of your hair," Dan said. "I get what happened here but they still have to do their jobs. I can't tell them to fuck off because you used to work for me."

"It's not a problem," I said.

"Are you sure that's all it was with him? He was afraid you'd talk about the affair?"

"I can't think of anything else," I lied.

Dan sat down on the couch next to me. "All right."

"All right," I said.

"You need anything else?" Dan asked Sarah.

"No. I'm done for now. I'll need to follow up later, but we can do that at the station."

Dan nodded. "Step outside and wait for me. I have some other questions for you."

Sarah put a hand on my shoulder and squeezed it. I managed not to shake her off. She gave me a sympathetic smile and left the house.

Dan sighed deeply and leaned back, putting his hands behind his head. "Well, this is a complete goatfuck."

I shrugged. "Seen worse," I said quietly.

Dan gave me a meaningful look. I knew where this was going and decided to try to head it off. "I'm fine, boss. It's not the first guy I've killed."

"I know that."

"It's not the second guy, either. Or the third."

"I know."

"The *Union-Tribune* was making noise about it even before…" I didn't want to say the name tonight. "Before my last case. Said the police department had hired their own executioner."

"That was bullshit."

"I don't know if it was."

"I do. I sent you after some really bad guys, and they didn't always come in easy. Your shoots were all clean. If any of them hadn't been I'd have brought you up on charges. You know that's true."

I smiled weakly at him. Honest Dan. He really would have,

too.

"I'm not sure what you want me to say right now," I told him.

"I want you to tell me how you're doing."

I eyed the vodka again, but didn't reach for it. "I hate this," I said quietly. "I hate that there was a dead guy on my floor just now and I'm the one that put him there. Okay? I fucking hate it."

"Okay."

"But I'm all right. You don't need to worry about me. I'm all right."

He glanced at the vodka. "You really call this all right, Nevada?"

"We're not getting into that tonight."

He sighed. "Fine. Not tonight. You've been through enough."

I reached out and patted his arm. It was as close to hugging him as I'd let myself get. "You didn't need to come," I said. "Sarah was doing fine."

"I didn't come to check on Sarah," he said.

"I know."

"Besides," he said. "It's not just me. *Everyone* came."

I frowned. "What do you mean, 'everyone came?'"

"Go look out the door."

I stood up, reaching instinctively for my vodka to take it along, but let my hand fall back empty. Not yet. I walked over to my open front door and looked outside. I had expected a few squad cars to be outside, and possibly the ambulance that had come earlier if they'd stuck around. But instead the street was full of SDPD cruisers, all with their lights flashing. They stretched all the way down the block in each direction, lining both sides of the street. There had to be fifty cops outside. Maybe more.

I took a few steps outside and looked up and down the street, trying to get a count of the cars. "What the hell?" I asked.

"Someone tried to kill a cop," Dan said from behind me. "This is what happens."

I glanced back at him. "I'm not a cop anymore."

He stepped forward and looked into my eyes. "You will always be a cop, Nevada."

Turning around, I saw that everyone was staring at me now. Nobody spoke. The silence was almost unbelievably awkward. Were they expecting me to make a speech? Wave? Dance a jig?

"What was that you asked me earlier at HQ?" Dan asked. "Wasn't it whether I thought there was anyone in that building who wanted to help you?"

"I think it was something like that," I said softly.

Dan sighed. "You're a fucking idiot, Nevada."

"I know," I admitted.

"What do you think about the Davies case?" he asked, just a little too suddenly.

Bad transition, I thought. He wasn't sure whether to believe me about Todd and wanted to see if I'd slip up now that I was off my guard. Not likely. "I think it's a domestic problem," I said. "I'll track Heather down and make sure she and the kid are all right. Shouldn't take more than a day or two."

"All right," Dan said. I wasn't sure if he believed me, but I hadn't really given him a reason not to. And if I was acting off, I was more than a little drunk right now.

"All right," I repeated. It seemed like we said that a lot, even though things were never really all right.

"I'm going to stick a couple uniforms on your house tonight," he told me.

"You don't need to…" I began, but then I caught myself. It would make him feel better, and he might get suspicious if I refused too strongly. "Just for tonight, okay? I don't think Todd has anyone coming to avenge him."

"Just tonight," he nodded. "And tomorrow I want you to come in and talk to someone about what happened here."

"Sarah will call me when she needs to follow up. I'll go in and talk to her then."

"Not about the…not about the investigation. I want you to sit with a department psychologist."

"Oh, for god's sake," I said. "I told you I'm fine."

"You spent six months in the psych ward," he said. "And some of that time was in a padded room. So I want you to talk to someone."

I sighed. Arguing with him now was going to get me nowhere. "I have a therapist."

"You seen her recently?"

"No."

"So go see her."

"Fine."

"Promise me."

"Fuck off," I said. "You already had a promise today."

He looked at me sternly. "Tell me you'll go see her."

"Fine."

"Say the whole sentence."

"I'll go see my therapist," I said.

"Okay."

I looked back at the street. "Can you get this riff-raff out of here?" I asked, waving at the assembled police cars. "My neighbors are going to be pissed."

"Your neighbors have the pleasure of living in the safest neighborhood in San Diego tonight," he said. "They should be happy."

"That will last about ten minutes," I said, "and then they'll start bitching about the parking."

"We'll be out of your hair soon."

"Okay. And, Dan?"

"Yeah?" he asked.

I looked at my feet. "Thanks for coming."

His brow wrinkled. "Did you really think I wouldn't?"

"No."

"People care about you, Nevada. As much as you've tried to shut yourself off from the rest of the world, we're still here."

"I know."

"Do you?" he asked, searching my face. "Do you know that?"

I looked away. "I'll show the CSI guys out when they're done. Then I'm going to bed."

He sighed. "Good night, Nevada."

"Good night." I left him on the doorstep and went back inside where CSI was finishing up. They had taped an outline of Todd's body onto the carpet where he had fallen. I didn't want to look at it.

I took a seat on my couch to wait, and now I did pick up the vodka. I wasn't going to drink it yet. I just wanted to hold it. At least, that was what I told myself. It turned out not to be true.

Chapter 9

I spent most of the night lingering in that little space between awake and asleep, the space I got trapped in when I hadn't had enough to drink to knock me out, but didn't have the wherewithal to get up and find more alcohol.

For a brief interval I dreamed. It was an old nightmare that I hadn't had in a long time. I was on my knees in the Laughing Man's abattoir, where I'd gone to confront him and save the two little girls that had been his last victims. I'd been too late, and now I was on my knees, my right wrist broken from where he'd smashed it with a crowbar. He'd hit me once in the knee as well, hard enough that I wouldn't be standing up for a while, and several times in the torso. Then he'd gone to work on me with his hands. I didn't know how much damage he'd done at the time, but I knew our fight was over.

In the end the Laughing Man stood over me, savoring his victory, savoring the end of our game, the straight razor in his hand poised to end me once and for all. I watched him through tears of pain and despair, waiting for him to do it. And then he'd just turned and walked away.

I knelt there, covered in my own blood, staring at my hands. My wrist had swelled up to twice its normal size, cutting the nerves off so I couldn't move the fingers on my right hand at all. Blood ran down my arms. I'd failed. I'd lost the game. The two little girls were dead, posed in his still-life with wide grins carved into their faces. It was the Laughing Man's signature mutilation. I stared at them in horror as physical pain and mental anguish wrestled each other for dominance over me.

And then I started to laugh.

At first it was only a giggle, one tiny giggle as my eyes focused on a single rivulet of blood running toward my elbow. It was followed by another giggle, and then another. And then I was laughing in earnest, laughing through the pain of my broken ribs, a high-pitched hysterical shrieking that continued as the goddamn backup I'd called for too late finally arrived. The other police officers thought I must have taken a blow to the head, but it was worse than that. I'd somehow taken a blow *inside* my head. Something in my brain had snapped and even then, in the midst of my hysteria, I knew it was something I wouldn't be able to put back together again. I was still laughing when the ambulance came, laughing while they drove me to the hospital, and I kept laughing right up until they shot me full of Thorazine.

I blinked and was back in my bedroom, the sun coming up outside. I looked at the clock and was surprised to find it was fairly early in the morning. The vodka I'd brought into the bedroom with me was still on the bedside table. I hadn't had nearly enough of it, obviously. Clearly not enough to keep the nightmare away.

My legs felt weak but not shaky as I stood up next to the bed. I picked up the vodka and looked at it for a moment, then took a small sip. I debated taking another, but put the bottle down instead. I wanted more, but I had things to do. Later I could crawl into a hole and die, if that was what I really wanted. But right now I had a case to solve.

The outline of Todd's body the CSI guys had taped down the night before was still on my living room carpet. I guess they expected me to clean it up myself. I looked at it for a moment, and then the strangest damn thing happened. I started to cry.

It only lasted for a few seconds, half a dozen heaving sobs, and then it was over. I rubbed my face clean of the few tears that had fallen. What the hell had that been about? I didn't cry. I *never* cried.

My stomach rumbled. That was unusual. I rarely had an appetite in the morning. But then again, I rarely had an appetite at all. I went into the kitchen to see what I had, unsurprised that it turned out to be next to nothing. I was going to have to settle for instant soup again. I put the water on to boil and made myself a cup.

I sipped the soup as I plotted my next move. I needed to talk to Alan Davies. If he didn't know his family had been abducted, he needed to know. If he knew that already, we were going to have a discussion about how telling lies has consequences.

Something wasn't sitting right with me, though. I thought about it as I sipped the soup. I had the feeling I was missing a big old obvious clue somewhere, but my brain was too fogged from alcohol abuse to work out what it was. I sighed. I'd figure it out eventually. I almost always did.

I finished up the soup, fairly certain I'd be able to keep it down. I'd pick up something more solid later on. It would be a nice change for my system, having the chance to digest real food.

Alan Davies's card was still in my pocket. I took it out and looked at the number, then put it away. I wasn't going to do this by phone. I'd go see him in person.

My clothes didn't smell all that great, but I didn't see much point in changing them. I didn't have anything else that was cleaner. I'd get some laundry done one of these days. Or maybe I'd just burn all of my clothes and buy new ones. That might actually be a better idea.

Outside I saw that the police had put up yellow crime scene tape around my yard. One more thing for me to clean up, but it could wait. Todd's Lincoln had been towed away sometime during the night. I wondered if Davies knew about the hit yet. I imagined it would have raised some questions when Todd didn't show up for work this morning. Or, more likely, Dan had called him last night and torn Davies a new asshole.

I had just put the key in the Mustang's ignition when I decided I wasn't ready to see Davies yet. That weird crying jag had been disturbing. I needed to see someone else first.

Pacific Beach, or PB as it was known to the locals, was about ten minutes north of my house on surface streets. PB was a place full of tourist bars, aging hippies, and grifters. I had no use for it, but the person I needed to see would probably be up there this morning. If she wasn't, her staff would be able to tell me where to find her.

Molly Malone's dojo sat in a small strip mall about a block from the beach. The rent on the place must have been astronomical, but I knew she operated the dojo at a small financial loss. Molly had made a small fortune in her therapist's practice, and later as a self-help author. She ran this place out of her love for karate, not to make a profit.

I spotted her standing in a corner of the dojo when I stepped inside. Molly stood at exactly five feet tall and might have weighed a hundred pounds soaking wet, provided she was also wearing an overcoat that was soaking wet. She was speaking with a lanky man in a Hawaiian shirt and a scarlet-haired woman in a leather jacket. That reminded me I had a leather jacket just like it hanging in my closet at home. I could wear that one instead of the one with the bullet hole in the arm. That might save me some awkward glances later.

Molly spotted me and her eyes lit up. She said goodbye to her visitors and came over to see me. I braced myself for the hug I knew was coming. People just couldn't stop hugging me these days.

She held on to me for a moment and gave me a quick kiss on the cheek. "You look awful," she said, pulling back to frown at me.

"Nice to see you, too," I said. I nodded at her guests. "Am I interrupting?"

"No," she said. She smiled gently at the man in the Hawaiian shirt as he passed by on his way to the door, the redhead trailing behind him. The man smiled sheepishly back at her.

"What was that about?" I asked.

"He asked if I knew any place they could buy some good seafood."

I winced. "First time you've heard that one?"

"It's not the first time I've heard that one this week," she said. "I'm thinking of writing a book of 'Molly Malone' jokes. But, no, they were looking for a friend of theirs. Actually, two, I guess. A guy and his cat. Something about…" she shrugged. "I don't know. It's Pacific Beach."

"Stranger things."

"Yeah. What are *you* doing here? You said you were done with therapy. And done with me, if I remember correctly."

I spotted an interesting crack on the floor and pretended to study it. That was the politest possible version of what I'd said to her the last time I'd seen her. "I think I said something like that," I admitted.

"Well then? What's going on? You didn't come to work out?"

"I doubt I could," I said. "I've been…pretty sick."

"Yeah," she nodded. "I can smell that you've been pretty sick. You've been sick for a long time, I think."

"Yeah." Now I'd spotted an interesting crack on the wall. I wanted to look anywhere but at her.

"What's going on, Nevada?"

I hadn't come here to lie to her, had I? It was time to come clean. "I…I killed someone last night."

I'd almost expected her to recoil, but Molly only nodded. "Okay. Are you hurt, Nevada?"

"No."

"Were you drunk?"

"I'm usually drunk," I admitted.

"How did it happen?"

"Ridge-hand to the throat. Crushed his windpipe."

"No, I meant…" Molly shook her head. "Nevada, you know I love you, but should you be speaking to an attorney instead of me right now? Because I'm going to have to call the police."

"Oh," I said, realizing what she was getting at. "No, it was self-defense. He came at me with a pistol. I had Dan Evans and half the SDPD at my house last night. It's okay."

"All right," she nodded. "Did you come here because you need to talk about it?"

"I don't know," I said. "I don't think so." What *had* I come here for? God, I was just hopeless, wasn't I? I had things I needed to be doing right now instead of having a meltdown.

Molly looked at me the way you look at a baby when it's thinking about taking its first steps. "Go get a *gi* out of the locker room," she said.

"What?"

"Go," she said. "There are some clean ones hanging on the guest rack. One of them will fit you."

I went into the locker room and took a white *gi* from the set Molly's staff loaned to prospective clients who wanted to try a session before they signed up and bought their own gear. I changed quickly, putting my own clothes in an unlocked locker. Anyone who wanted them badly enough to tolerate the stink deserved to have them. I fastened the *gi* with a white belt. I had my own black belt at home along with a *gi* I'd had custom made for me, but they were probably growing moldy under a pile of garbage. Someday I'd find them, and maybe burn them along with the rest of my old clothes.

Molly was waiting for me in a corner of the dojo when I came out. She bowed sharply as I approached her. "Defend yourself," she said. Then, without even bothering to square off, she came at me.

Even on my best day I'd have been no match for her. When I was healthy I'd been very good, and I'd earned my black belt honestly, but Molly was some kind of karate savant. She spent ten minutes toying with me, launching attacks I could just barely defend against, and shrugging off any attempt I made to counter. Finally I collapsed, drenched with sweat and breathing harder than I could remember ever breathing before.

Molly fetched a small trash can and put it down in front of me. "Here," she said. "You're going to need this."

"Why?" I panted. Then I started retching. The remains of my noodle soup and vodka breakfast were in the trash can a moment later.

Molly was good enough to hold my unwashed, unbrushed hair back as I vomited. When it was over I looked up and saw a group of green-belts watching us in horror. They must have assumed Molly had landed a good punch in my gut. The truth was she'd never hit me at all. The exertion alone had been enough to wreck me.

She took the trash can away when she was sure I was done heaving and handed me a bottle of water. "Sip it slowly," she commanded. I took two sips, the cool water a relief as it went down my throat. Molly watched me approvingly. "Good," she said. "Now stand up."

"Why?"

"We're not done."

This time she did hit me. Not hard enough to hurt me, but enough that I'd remember having been in here when I woke up tomorrow. I didn't do much better with my attacks than in the session before, never coming close to making contact with her, but at least not missing by enough to completely humiliate myself in the process.

We went at it for another ten minutes until I collapsed, my legs shaking from a combination of withdrawal and exhaustion. "That's enough," Molly said.

"Jesus *fucking* Christ," I wheezed.

Molly sat down next to me, crossing her legs. She offered me the bottle of water again, which I took eagerly. "That was pathetic, sweetheart," she said.

"I know," I said. I drank the water, gulping too quickly. A wave of nausea hit me, but I managed not to vomit this time.

"You all right?"

"Not really. You could have gone a little easier on me."

"Oh, Nevada," she sighed. "You can't do anything the easy way. Come on." She stood up.

I put a hand up in surrender. "No more. Please."

"No, we're done. Time for the sauna."

Molly half-supported and half-dragged me as we went into

93

the locker room. My *gi* was drenched with sweat and as I took it off I was a little surprised to find that my body smelled like stale vodka. It was nearly enough to get me retching again.

We went into a small, wood-paneled sauna adjacent to the women's locker room. It was early in the day and we had it to ourselves. Molly had gone to the juice bar and come back with two large bottles of water, more than I typically drank in a month. "Time to sweat," she said, handing me one of them.

Inside the sauna, Molly poured a ladle full of water onto the hot stones and we sat there as the heat overwhelmed us. "I've never sweat this much in my life" I told her.

"Good," she said. "It'll get some of that poison out of you."

"I'm not sure that's how it works," I said.

"Can't hurt."

We sat on the benches and sweated in silence for a moment. The heat did feel good, and the cool water was like drinking from a river in Heaven, but I still couldn't help but notice how *wrong* my own sweat smelled. I'd known I was pretty far from healthy, but that had been unexpected.

"Ridge-hand," Molly noted. "A little unorthodox for Shotokan."

"It was the best move I had available," I said. "I wasn't trying to kill the guy. I just wanted to end the fight."

"A shot to the throat is always tricky," she said. "It'll stop anyone in their tracks, no matter how big they are. But a little too hard…"

"Yeah."

"So tell me what happened."

I told her the story of how Chandler Emerson had showed up on my doorstep and taken me to Solana Beach to hear Alan Davies make an offer I couldn't refuse. I told her about my confrontation with Dan Evans at the police station, and my trip to Heather Davies's condo and what I'd seen there. And then I walked her through Todd's arrival at my house, and his subsequent death at my hands.

She nodded frequently throughout the story, sipping occasionally from her huge bottle of water as she listened. When I was finished she was silent for a long moment. I kept sweating and let her think about it. "I should never have agreed to be your therapist," she said finally.

"I'm that much trouble?"

"You are, but that's not what I meant and you know it, Nevada. I can be your therapist or your friend. Not both. I took you on as a patient because I knew you'd never see anyone else and I thought if you had some professional help…" she shook her head. "Well, look where that got us."

"It's not that bad…" I began.

"You look like the corpse of my friend Nevada," she cut me off. "Not my friend Nevada. Drink some water."

I didn't have the energy to fight with her. I drank some water.

"As your therapist, I should tell you to get far away from all of this. Get yourself into a rehab, get yourself some *intensive* treatment, because goddamn, Nevada, you really need it. You need it more than anyone I have ever met."

I nodded. That was more or less what I'd expected her to

say. "And since you know that's never going to happen?"

She sighed. "Work the case. Go find the woman and her daughter. Try not to kill anyone else."

"I didn't mean to kill him!"

"I believe that. I also believe there's a very thin line between where you are right now and complete, never-coming-back insanity. Did you notice how I didn't say the line was between sanity and insanity?"

"Yeah, I saw what you did there."

"It's because you're *not* sane, Nevada," she continued. "You're very sick. You haven't crossed that line yet, but you're so close…tell me something. If you were in a situation where you had to kill an innocent person to get to the Laughing Man, would you do it?"

"This has nothing to do with the Laughing Man."

"*Everything* with you is about the Laughing Man," she said. "Would you kill someone if it meant getting to him?"

I should have pretended to struggle with the question, but I knew exactly what I'd have done. "Yes. I would."

She nodded. "Of course you would. See, that's the *wrong* answer. You can't see this right now, but the way you're thinking? It's really screwed up."

"And you think working a case is going to help me with my thinking? Dan had the same idea."

"Dan has a tragic romantic streak, but I don't think he's all that far off. Sitting home alone drinking is not doing anything to get you back on the right path. You're…I don't know how to say this."

"I'm a cop?"

"No. Being a cop doesn't matter. It's just a convenient outlet. You have this pathological need for opposition. You're a...you're a *hunter*. You need to be out hunting or you're not happy."

A hunter? I'd heard that before, but not from Molly. Years ago a psychiatrist who'd fancied himself a real-life Hannibal Lecter had said it to me as I'd pushed him into a squad car. He'd killed two people before I caught up with him, and when I had him in cuffs he decided he wanted to analyze me on the drive to jail. That had been a very long twenty minutes. If anybody had seen me slam him into a wall once we got to the police station, nobody had said anything about it.

"So go hunt," Molly continued. "It'll satisfy whatever part of you needs to do that, and maybe bring you a little closer to our side of the line."

"And then I'll be sane?" I smirked.

"No," she said. "I don't think you're ever going to be sane. Not really. But if we straighten you out a little, get you to stop self-medicating, maybe you'll have an easier time making the right choices when the time comes."

I sighed deeply. I wasn't sure what I'd wanted to hear when I'd come here, but I was pretty sure that wasn't it. "Is that your professional opinion?"

"No. That is your friend's opinion. My professional opinion is that I should fifty-one fifty your ass." 5150 was the section of California state code that allowed for putting an involuntary psychiatric hold on someone who was deemed a danger to themselves or to others. It meant 72 hours locked in a psych ward.

"That didn't work out so well last time," I pointed out.

"No," she said. "It didn't. Finish your water."

We sat there and kept sweating for a while, me drinking as much water at a time as I could without getting nauseous. After a while Molly asked, "You already know what you're going to do when you leave here. Why don't you tell me about it?"

"I'm going to work the case," I said. "It is good, to be out there doing something useful again. It makes me feel…I don't know. Like my life matters."

"Of course your life matters," Molly said. "It matters whether you're working cases or not."

"I don't know."

Molly sighed. "Nevada, I have to ask. Have you thought about A.A.?"

I nearly choked on my water. "Are you serious?"

"I am."

"You think I want to sit around and listen to a bunch of losers whine about how much they miss drinking?"

"I think you'd find that's not what twelve-step programs are about."

"No."

"They have meetings for cops. You'd be talking to people that have had similar experiences…" she cut herself off. "No, I guess that's not true. But cops. There's at least some common ground there."

"I really don't see the point."

"Will you come back and talk to me about it when you finish with this case?"

"As my friend or as my therapist?"

"As your friend who happens to be a therapist," she said. "Not your therapist. I could recommend someone else for that. I know a guy…"

"I'll talk to you about it later," I cut her off.

"Promise me a year isn't going to go by before I see you again?"

"Molly…"

"Promise me."

"Fine," I said. "I promise. Jesus. Everyone and their damn promises these days."

"We're going to save your life, Nevada. Mark my words."

I didn't reply. I just would have told her my life wasn't worth saving, and then we'd have had to go round and round again. We'd been there and done that before. But I was glad I'd come to see Molly. I was going to have some bruises in the morning, but I'd be proud of them. I'd *earned* them. Even if Molly hadn't made me promise, I'd have come back to see her. I missed her. I missed a lot of things.

I missed my life.

Chapter 10

After a long shower I found myself wishing I had some clean clothes to put on. The smell of the clothes I'd worn to the gym made me nauseous. I didn't want to drive home and do laundry, but there was no way I could keep this shirt on much longer.

There was a novelty t-shirt store for tourists two doors up from Molly's dojo. I went inside and picked out the first shirt that didn't make me want to punch someone. It had a cartoon of a surfing dog on it, which was not my thing at all, but at least it was clean.

I changed shirts in my car and tossed the dirty one onto the back seat. That would do for now. New jeans and underwear could wait for a while.

Alan Davies's card was still in my pocket. I retrieved it and then remembered I still had no idea where my cell phone was. I'd never bothered to look for it after Todd had shown up at my house and tried to kill me. It hardly seemed worth driving back to Ocean Beach to make a phone call to let him know I was coming. I'd just have to show up unannounced. Davies would have to make the time to see me, provided he was home and not off at some gangster business meeting. Was that something gangsters did? Go to meetings?

My hands were starting to tremble when I reached for the steering wheel and I realized my body was lacking both food and alcohol now. I never ate that much anyway, but having vomited earlier meant I had been running on empty for quite a while. I needed to get some calories in me before my body started to shut down.

I drove north as far as Del Mar before stopping at a fast food place and hitting the drive-through. As I was waiting for a hamburger, I realized something was still nagging me. I was missing something. Working a case could be a lot like doing a jigsaw puzzle. Sometimes you were missing pieces, but I had the feeling I was missing a piece I'd already seen and just misplaced somewhere. It was starting to drive me nuts.

Kidnappers, since that seemed to be what I was dealing with, had posed as furniture delivery people and wheeled two huge crates into the lobby of a security building, past the guard, and right up to the door of Heather Davies's condo. And she'd let them in? That didn't make any sense. She'd have known perfectly well that she hadn't ordered any furniture and wasn't expecting a delivery. Why would she have let them in? Getting furniture delivered wasn't like having someone send you flowers. It was never a surprise.

I thought about that as I ate, burger in one hand and the other on the wheel as I drove. She wouldn't have had to let them in. She'd only have had to open the door. The kidnappers could have forced their way inside easily enough. In that building it would have been hard to hear if your neighbor screamed.

The security guard in front of Davies's estate was the same guy I'd seen before, but this time he was openly carrying an MP5. "Jesus," I said as he approached my window. "Seriously?"

"Ma'am?"

"Are you guys expecting a war?"

"You can go on up, ma'am." The gate was already opening up behind him.

I drove through the gate and started on up towards Davies's house, which was just as garish as I remembered. As I approached the fountain out front I could see Davies on his lawn, hurrying toward the gazebo. He was wearing a different Tommy Bahama outfit. I was starting to wonder if he ever wore anything else.

He wanted to talk in the gazebo again? Was he afraid I was going to stink up his house? Given my appearance yesterday it would have been a reasonable conclusion, but...

Of course that wasn't it, I realized. And he wasn't afraid I was going to steal an ashtray or make fun of his furniture, either.

I pulled the car off to the side of the driveway and got out, not bothering to shut my door. Davies was still making a beeline for the gazebo. "Hey!" I yelled after him. "Davies! Asshole!"

Davies turned to face me once he reached the gazebo. He took a small, square device out of his pocket and pressed a switch on it. I couldn't see it well enough to identify it, but I was pretty sure I already knew what it was.

I wasn't thrilled about the long walk to the gazebo, especially after my exercise earlier, but I hardly had a choice at this point. He wasn't going to come to me. "You son of a bitch," I said once I reached him.

Davies put his hands up. "I understand you're…"

I punched him in the solar plexus as hard as I could, which really wasn't all that hard given how tired I was. It felt like punching a brick wall, sending a shock wave up my arm all the way into my shoulder. Davies fell to his knees with a grunt. I would have to hope he stayed down and didn't try to challenge me. I didn't have another punch left over.

"You fucking lied to me!" I shouted.

Davies made it to one knee, his face red. I pulled back as if I was going to hit him again, and he put a hand up in surrender. "Damn it," he wheezed. I understood the sentiment. My arm had gone numb.

"You knew they'd been kidnapped," I said. "That small army you've got walking around here with assault rifles isn't normal at all, is it? You're getting ready for a war."

"Yes."

"Son of a bitch!" I repeated. The truth was I was angrier at myself than I was at him. I should have seen through him from the start. If I hadn't been drinking myself to sleep every night for the last few years I would have.

"Can I get up now?" he asked.

I took a step back and nodded, hoping he wasn't going to try to make a move. He'd be able to beat me pretty easily now if he did. I wasn't sure I could lift my right arm if I tried.

Davies got to his feet and kept both hands in the air with his palms facing outward. "Can we sit down?"

"You first," I said.

He sat and put his hands on the table. I hesitated a moment, then took the seat across from him.

"That thing in your pocket is some kind of jammer isn't it? You're worried about bugs."

He nodded. "The house is too big to sweep every day. This spot isn't. And this," he tapped his pocket, "creates enough interference to make most bugs useless, but it has a very short range. Not much bigger than this pagoda."

"Okay. Tell me everything."

"Chandler will be here in…"

"I do not care about Chandler," I cut him off. "You seriously want to start talking now."

He took a deep breath. "It started…well, nearly two weeks ago now," he said. "I got a call that my family had been taken."

"Who called you?"

"I don't have any names. I don't know who they are. The man has a Mexican accent. Probably some competitor of mine."

"What did they ask for?"

"Money. Two million dollars."

I scoffed. "That's it? You fucking moron. Pay them. Pay them all of it right now and get your family back."

"You don't understand," Davies said. "The two million was due in three days. I *did* pay it. Then they called again and asked for two million more, due in three more days. Then it was two million more three days after that. I paid every time, but it just continues."

Ransom on an installment plan? "Until when?"

"There isn't any 'when.' There is no timeline. I guess until I don't have any money left. Then I don't know what happens."

I thought that over. I'd never heard of it before, but I had to admit it made sense. In the movies you always saw kidnappers making absurd demands, like twenty million dollars in 24 hours. That was next to impossible to actually pull off. That much money simply couldn't be obtained and transferred that quickly. Even for the very rich it takes time to liquidate assets. Nobody keeps that much cash sitting around their house.

I heard footsteps on the grass. Chandler Emerson was rushing toward the pagoda. "Oh, boy," I said. "Now the party can get started."

Emerson glared at me as he went to take a third chair at the table. "Sir, I wish you hadn't started without me," he said to Davies.

"I didn't make an appointment," I said.

Emerson turned to me, his face stern. "You are Mr. Davies's employee. You should have called in advance…" he began.

"You know what?" I addressed Davies. "Get rid of this fucking guy."

Emerson started to bluster but I kept my eyes fixed on Davies. "Now," I said.

Davies turned to Emerson. "It's all right, Chandler," he said softly. "Give us a minute, will you?"

"Sir, I really think…"

"Shoo, Chandler," I said, waving him away like he was a fly ruining my picnic.

Chandler's eyes shot murder at me but he stepped out of the pagoda and took up a position a few feet away. "Farther, Chandler!" I yelled, not looking at him. I saw him take a few more steps backward out of the corner of my eye.

"Is that really necessary?" Davies asked me.

'You're number one on my shitlist right now," I said. "Maybe you don't want to ask me what's really necessary."

"Fair enough."

"How are these payments working?"

"He transfers the money…" Emerson called.

"Back the fuck up, Chandler!"

Chandler took another step back. "You tell me," I said to Davies.

"They call after I make a transfer. The Mexican puts Heather on the phone. Then he tells me when to make the next transfer and hangs up."

"You've talked to Heather?"

"She never gets more than a sentence out before they stop her."

I thought about it. "Does she say the same thing every time they call?"

He frowned. "I...I don't think so." His eyes widened when he realized why I'd asked the question. "Do you think it's a recording?"

"I don't know. What about Anna?"

"They don't let me talk to Anna."

"Okay," I said. I thought it over. "You know your boy Todd tried to kill me last night?"

"Dan Evans called and told me about it," he said. "I'm sorry about that."

"You know why he did it?"

"Dan said there had been affair and you found out about it."

"Did you know about the affair?"

"Not until last night."

"I lied to Dan," I said. "Todd was there to kill me, but he was acting on somebody else's orders. He was being threatened."

"Good god!"

"Whoever he was working for was going to tell you about the affair if he didn't kill me."

"I see."

I cocked my head at him. "I can't help but notice how surprised you aren't."

"It doesn't surprise me that one of my people would be working with, or for, the kidnappers, no."

"That's the real reason why you don't have your own

people working on this. What, you don't exactly inspire loyalty?"

"They're employees," Davies said. "Other than Chandler and a few others, I don't trust any of them. Someone makes a better offer, they take it. It's like any other job."

"But Wal-Mart isn't going to shoot you in the head if you leave to go work at Best Buy."

He nodded. "No, I suppose they aren't."

I glanced at Emerson, who was still fuming a few yards away. "This explains why you went to Dan."

"Yes. Traditional law enforcement wasn't going to touch this."

"And why you lied to me."

"What would you have said if I'd told you the truth?"

"I'd have told you to go fuck yourself."

"Of course you would have."

"But knowing I'd find out the truth, and putting me in danger at the same time, that was kind of clever."

"I didn't mean to put you in danger!" he protested.

"Of course you did," I said. "It's a kidnapping. I was in danger the minute I started looking for your family. But you were banking on that. If someone took a shot at me and I survived, I'd probably be pissed off enough about it to go after whoever it was. And if I didn't survive, Dan Evans would tear the city apart looking for whoever killed me. It's a win-win for you."

Davies opened his mouth, shut it, then opened it again. "I

hadn't thought of it exactly like that, but you're right."

"It wasn't the best plan in the world," I said. "If I'd died, Dan would have taken you apart when he was finished with whoever had done me."

"But my family would be safe."

I nodded. That much was probably true.

We sat there in silence as I mulled it over. I wanted to take my frustration out on someone, and Emerson was standing *right there*, but in the end I took the high road.

"When is the next transfer scheduled?"

"Tomorrow at two. It's always at two."

"I'll be here for it."

His eyes widened. "You'll still help me?"

"I'm in it now," I said. "I won't let a child die if there's anything I can do about it. But I swear to god, if you lie to me again, I'll put a bullet in you when this is done."

"I promise. You'll know everything I know from now on."

"Good," I said. I stood up. "I'll be back tomorrow."

"What are you going to do?"

"Honestly?" I asked. "I'm probably going to go have a drink. Then we'll see."

Chapter 11

I had a lot to think about on the way back to San Diego. The question of who had ordered Todd to kill me was at the forefront of my mind. Whoever was behind the kidnapping had put the fear in him, but how could they have found out about the affair? Well, in all honesty, Todd hadn't struck me as much of a master of subterfuge. You could probably buy him a few drinks in a bar and he'd open up like a Christmas present.

Or someone could be listening in. There was no shortage of people who might try to get a bug into Davies's house, the FBI and the SDPD being at the top of my list of suspects. Maybe somebody had gotten greedy. It wouldn't be entirely unheard of for someone in law enforcement to hear something interesting on a wiretap and try to make a little money off of it, but going so far as to kidnap a woman and her child? That would be a new one for me. I had contacts I could reach out to in order to find out if Davies was the subject of an active investigation, and if so who was running it, but it meant showing my face in front of even more people, and lately I'd felt like a baby panda at the zoo. It didn't seem worth it.

One of Davies's competitors seemed more likely. If you wanted to bleed him dry, taking his family hostage seemed like a good way to do it. And flipping one of Davies's people to find out about the affair was just a matter of choosing the right one to approach, and having the right amount of cash to offer.

The next call from the kidnappers wasn't until tomorrow afternoon, so at least I had some time to think about things. With a little luck this would make more sense once I'd had more time to think about it.

When I got back to my house I parked at the curb again. I sat in the car for a moment, checking the mirrors. Nobody was approaching. If someone else was going to try to take a shot at me, they weren't showing themselves yet.

I got out of the car and looked up and down the street. Everything was clear. I felt like an idiot for being as nervous as I was, but I'd earned that paranoia, hadn't I?

My front door seemed suddenly very far away, and I found myself wanting my gun back. I could have asked Dan for one last night. He might have gone for it. He would have had to weigh the odds that I'd use it for protection against the chance I'd put it in my mouth and pull the trigger. I'm not sure what conclusion he would have reached. I honestly wasn't sure what I'd have done with a gun, either. On a bad enough day, or if I was in a blackout…

Inside the house I poured myself an inch of vodka and sat down on the couch to think. Everything I knew about working a kidnapping case I'd seen on television. That wasn't going to be particularly useful in real life. Not unless I rounded up everyone in Davies's study and somehow got the kidnapper to say something *only he would know*. And then maybe daisies would fly out of my ass. That seemed about equally as likely.

I thought about calling Dan Evans and coming clean about what was really going on. As much as I wanted to talk to him, I was almost certain he would call either the organized crime unit or the FBI as soon as he was done yelling at me. I could take the yelling, but damned if I was going to give up on this case.

Out of curiosity I switched on the television. I wasn't entirely surprised to find that my cable had been shut off. I had no idea the last time I had paid the bill, but it hadn't been recently. I needed to take a little of the cash Davies had given me and put it in the bank. I sipped my vodka. It could wait until tomorrow.

My head was a jumble of thoughts, too much so to think straight. I glanced at my vodka. I could either drink the rest of this, or try to be productive for a little while. I decided to give productivity a shot.

I went into my garage and looked at my motorcycle. It had been such a long time since I'd ridden it, and I was a little surprised to feel a sudden pang of longing to get on it and take it out onto the street. The bike was in no shape to ride, of course, but I pressed the starter anyway and wasn't surprised to find that the battery was dead. I knew I had a portable battery charger around here somewhere. And fresh oil? I had that too, didn't I? I probably had everything I needed to get the bike running.

It took me a little digging to find it, but I eventually got a battery charger hooked up to the bike. After that I found an oil pan and a couple bottles of fresh oil. I'd been doing my own bike maintenance since I was a teenager. None of this was new to me, but it felt fresh in a way that I liked. It was like rediscovering a much-loved hobby you had somehow forgotten about.

I found some rags and wiped the bike down when I was finished with the fluids. The tire pressure was fine. It would take a while for the battery to be ready but I could probably ride tomorrow if I wanted to. Provided that I was sober enough.

Back in my living room I started pulling the crime scene tape off of my carpet and walls. If anyone needed to remember where Todd had fallen, I could point it out easily enough, and the bullet holes were plain to see. I wasn't sure what I was going to do about that yet. I'd have to call the Harrisons about the damage. I'd pay for the repairs myself, but I was pretty sure having a guy choke to death in the living room of a house you owned did something bad to the property value. They might have some trouble selling it, if they ever wanted to.

I stuffed the bits of tape into a garbage bag and then went into my bedroom to clean. I wound up filling two bags and hauling them out to the dumpster. If I kept this up I was going to fill the dumpster before too long. I couldn't remember when trash pickup day was; it had been a long time since I'd bothered to perform that weekly ritual. I'd have to watch and see when the neighbors did theirs.

With all of that done and my house beginning to look marginally livable again, I planted myself on my couch and sipped my vodka as I thought things over. I was no closer to figuring out what my next move should be, but at least my house smelled better.

I took another swallow of vodka and laid my head back on

the couch. It felt like it had been a hundred years since I'd slept. I'd exercised, had a kind-of therapy session, done housework, and punched a gangster. And all of that before five o'clock. Back in the day that really wouldn't have seemed like so much, but with my health what it was now, I was exhausted. I felt like I'd run two marathons without a break in between.

I shut my eyes and allowed myself a deep sigh. I just needed a minute to...

Chapter 12

It was still light outside when I woke up, but the sun was in a different place and I realized it was morning. My clock said 8:32. I'd somehow gotten blasted enough to sleep through the night. Or maybe I'd just been that tired.

At some point during the night I'd retrieved my bottle of vodka from the kitchen and gone through the majority of it. That wasn't a surprise, historically speaking. What was surprising was that I'd stood the bottle upright on the arm of the couch and it had stayed there all night without spilling. I didn't usually have that much dexterity when I was in a blackout.

I stood up and almost instantly fell back down onto the couch, dizzy. I was going to need a minute. I wasn't sure how much I'd wound up drinking, but it clearly had been quite a bit more than I needed.

There was about a half inch of vodka left in the bottle. I picked it up and downed the last of it. No reason to let it go to waste.

Had I opened a second bottle last night? It felt like it. I could do an inventory later. Right now I needed to…

I woke up again and looked at the clock. 8:53. I'd only been out another twenty minutes, then. My head felt full of cobwebs and my mouth was dry. I thought about trying to drink some water, but the thought made me nauseous. Diet soda was going to have to do it.

My eyes caught sunlight as I stood up and I had to shield them with my hand. I never got hangovers, but it did seem especially bright out today. I had sunglasses around here somewhere. I'd find them before I left.

In the kitchen I was surprised to find that in my blackout I'd retrieved a legal pad from one of my closets and written a single word on it. "DELIVERY." What the hell was that supposed to mean? Had I been watching QVC and gone nuts ordering things? No, of course not. My television didn't work. So it was something else. I'd figure it out when I could think straight again.

I opened a can of diet soda and downed half of it an about two seconds, being rewarded with a loud belch for my trouble. Nice. I was the kind of girl all the boys wanted to take home to meet their mothers.

I went back into the living room and sat on the couch, shutting my eyes once again. I had some time to spare yet. I could stand to sleep just a little bit more.

It was nearly eleven when I woke up again. I rubbed my eyes and thought about that. I had three hours until Davies was supposed to make the next wire transfer to the kidnappers. That gave me time to do some other things I'd been neglecting.

I stripped off the clothes I was wearing and put them in the washing machine, along with an assortment of other things I gathered off my bedroom floor. If I put the machine on the quick cycle, everything should be done by the time I got out of the shower.

I didn't have enough energy to stand up in the shower, so I wound up huddling on the floor as the water poured down on me. This time I even washed my hair, which I hadn't bothered with two days ago. If I was lucky I'd be able to get a brush through it.

When my clothes were finished in the washer I stuffed them into the dryer and set it for the hottest setting. I didn't have anything I needed to worry about shrinking in there. I was just desperate to wear something that was actually clean, and that didn't have a cartoon dog on the front of it.

My hair didn't take well to brushing and I got bored with it somewhere at the point between rat's nest and bedhead. What the hell did it matter, anyway? I wasn't going up to Solana Beach on a date.

My clothes weren't as dry as I'd have liked when I took them out of the dryer, but Solana Beach was a good half hour away and I didn't plan to be driving fast. I shouldn't be driving at all, honestly, but I didn't think showing up at a gangster's house in a taxi was the best idea in the world.

The trip to Solana Beach was slow but uneventful. I felt like shit but I kept the car in my lane and below the speed limit. The guard out front didn't even bother to stop me this time. The gate was already opening as I approached and he waved me on through as if we were old friends. I actually waved back, then wondered if that was something people typically did here.

People who worked in an office complex might expect a friendly wave, but did the armed guards at a gangster's estate?

I could see Davies and Emerson sitting at the pagoda when I got out of the Mustang. I started for them, but suddenly lurched forward and vomited noisily on the grass. The retching was over in the blink of an eye, my nausea gone as quickly as it had come. I wiped my mouth with the back of my hand and looked up. Davies didn't seem to have noticed. Emerson had. From his expression you might have thought I'd just taken a dump in his mouth.

I made it to the pagoda without further incident. "We have to stop meeting like this," I said to Emerson. He scowled at me. On the table in front of him he had a laptop computer with a wireless modem plugged into one of the ports. In the center of the table sat a UPS envelope that had been torn open. A small, cheap-looking cell phone sat next to it.

"You didn't mention this before," I said. "I thought the kidnappers called the house."

"They did," said Davies. "This is new."

"Was there a note?"

"No. Just the phone."

Something had changed, then. Why were the kidnappers switching things up now? Because they knew I was involved? That seemed overly cautious. I was next to useless, after all.

I picked up the phone and flipped it open. It was as simple as they came. It would do voice calls and texts, but that was it.

"Typical burner," I said, putting it down. You could buy them by the dozen in any gas station in California. "Fully charged. You turned it on?"

"Yes," Davies said. "I guess there was no point in dusting it for fingerprints?" He looked unsure. He wanted me to tell him he hadn't done anything wrong.

"Anybody who went to this much trouble wouldn't have left anything behind we could use," I told him, thinking of the different things the Laughing Man had sent me over the years. "You did fine." Well, he'd nearly done fine. He hadn't put out anything for us to drink, and today my mouth was Gobi Desert dry.

He sighed. "I'm glad you're here," he said. "It feels good to have someone helping us who knows about these things."

"I worked homicide, not kidnappings," I reminded him.

"You're still a detective. We're not. I'm sorry I wasn't straight with you earlier. I should have been."

"If you had been I wouldn't be here now," I said. "We're past that."

"Okay."

"So how does this work?" I asked.

Emerson finished whatever he'd been doing on the laptop and slid it over to Davies. "It's ready for your password, sir."

Davies looked at his watch. "It's time."

I stood up and nearly lost my balance, needing to grip the edge of the table to catch myself. I wasn't sure if either of them noticed my slip, but neither man reacted. I came around to Davies's side of the table and looked over his shoulder. The computer's Internet browser was set to a bank's website, about to initiate a wire transfer. It wasn't a system I had ever seen before. "Tell me what this is," I said.

"Bank of Nevis," Davies said.

"Mr. Davies holds offshore accounts in several countries," Emerson said. "I wouldn't expect that's something you'd be familiar with."

"Banks in the Caribbean are often used to hide the assets of people who don't want questions asked about their income," I said. "Besides offering lower tax rates, they won't comply with requests for information from the U.S. government."

"Well, yes," Emerson said. "It's a bit more complicated than that, of course…"

"Do you want me to teach you?" I offered. I was bluffing, of course. Everything I'd just said I'd seen in a movie once.

"That's all right, Nevada," Davies said. He gave Emerson a warning look. "Let's try to remember we're all on the same side here."

"Of course," said Emerson.

"Do you want us to shake hands?" I asked Davies. "Because I'm not going to."

"Never mind," he said.

I looked at the numbers on the laptop's screen. If I understood it correctly, Davies was about to transfer two million dollars from his account into another, which was identified only by a sixteen-digit number. "What happens now?"

"I put in my password to confirm the transfer, click once there," he pointed at the screen, "and it's done."

"What about the other number?" I asked. It was of a different length than Davies's account number. "That's not a

Nevis account."

"It's a Swiss bank," Emerson said. "I was able to work out the identity of the bank based on the format, but it's a numbered account. That means…"

"That means there is no name attached to it," I finished.

"Correct."

I nodded. Numbered accounts were a particular favorite of drug lords, third world dictators, and anyone else who wanted to hide a large amount of money anonymously. Even the President of the bank where the money was being held might not know exactly who owned that account. More than that, there was likely no way he *could* figure it out. And even that only mattered if the money stayed put, which it wouldn't. A smart kidnapper would have the resources to divide up the money and transfer it to a dozen destinations around the globe. And then a dozen more. In a matter of hours it could be made to vanish into the digital ether, never to be found by even the most determined investigator.

I watched the screen for a moment, but couldn't think of any reason not to go ahead with the transfer. "All right," I said. "You may as well do it."

Davies typed for a moment and then clicked on the button he'd pointed out earlier. I saw a confirmation come up on the laptop's screen. "It's done," Davies said.

I went around and took my seat at the table again. "How long does a wire transfer like that take?" I asked.

"It's international," Emerson said. "But fifteen minutes at the outside."

"It's never been longer than that before we get the call,"

Davies said.

We sat there for a moment, none of us speaking. I had never liked long silences and tended to fill the gaps with wisecracks, but I had no energy left to do so now. Years of abusing my body, coupled with yesterday's exercise and whatever the hell I'd had to drink last night had taken their toll. I wanted to crawl under a rock and die.

"Remember to get both of them on the phone this time," I said to Davies. "Insist on it. Ask Heather what today's date is."

"Why?"

"So we know they're not playing a recording of her," I said. "Remember?"

"Of course," he said. "Today's date."

The cell phone chirped on the table. Davies's hand shot for it, flipping it open easily with his thumb. "Speakerphone," I told him. He looked at the phone's keypad in confusion, then pressed a button on the phone's side.

"Hello?" he asked.

"Mr. Davies," a man's husky voice said. I was no expert on accents, but his sounded like Baja California to me. I'd heard it before, or at least something very close to it, on my trips into Mexico.

"Let me talk to my wife," Davies said.

A moment passed and I could hear two men murmuring to each other in Spanish. It was muffled as if one of them was pressing his hand over the phone's receiver, but not quite firmly enough to block all the sound. One of the men sounded nervous, but I'd never learned enough Spanish to follow a conversation. It had been on my to-do list for…about fifteen years.

Emerson frowned at the phone. "Is this normal?" I asked him.

"No," Emerson said, his brow furrowed in worry. "They usually put Mrs. Davies on right away."

"What's wrong?" Davies asked. He looked at me for help. "What's wrong, Nevada?"

The hand was taken off the phone on the other end of the call and a little girl's voice came over the speaker. "Daddy?"

"Oh my god!" Davies cried. "Anna! Honey, I'm here!"

"Daddy," she said again, "Mommy's…" then there was a high-pitched cry as someone pulled the phone away from the girl, or pulled the girl away from the phone. One or the other. Anna screamed one more time, much farther from the phone now, and the man's voice was back.

"Three days, two million dollars. Same time." Then the connection dropped.

"What the hell was that?" Davies asked me, frantic.

I glanced over at Emerson, who looked stricken. He knew it, too. Well, one of us was going to have to tell Davies. Might as well be me.

"I'm sorry," I said, "but your wife is dead."

Chapter 13

Davies stared at me in confusion. "What are you talking about?"

"They killed her," I said. "I don't know why, but it's the only explanation for that phone call. They know they fucked up, but they still want your money. That's why they put Anna on the phone."

Davies shook his head and looked to Emerson for help. "Chandler? They killed her?"

Emerson bit his lip. "I'm sorry, sir, but I am forced to agree with her interpretation of events. It's the only thing that makes sense to me."

"She could have been hurt," Davies suggested. "Maybe she couldn't talk for some reason. If they'd...drugged her, maybe to keep her quiet?"

"Anything's possible," I told him, "but I don't think it's likely. She might have been trying to get away..."

"She wouldn't leave Anna."

"Then maybe she tried to fight the kidnappers. She could have overheard their plans. Maybe she took Anna and made a run for it. I don't know."

"Dead?" Davies asked. "Dead." He stood up and turned his back to us, stepping off the pagoda onto the lawn. He took a few steps and stopped, putting his hands on his hips. I could see he was breathing hard, trying to keep his emotions in check. Men who had gotten to his position didn't cry in front of other people. That just wouldn't do.

Emerson started to stand up. I put a hand on his arm. "Give him a minute," I said. He glared at me and shook my hand off. "You don't need to like me," I said, "but just trust me on this one, all right? He needs a minute to himself. I've done this kind of thing before. I've done it a lot." I could have elaborated, but that was all Emerson needed to know about me.

He hesitated for a moment, then sank back down in his seat. We waited as Davies paced around the lawn. His body language was making a journey from shock and sadness to anger. I'd seen this before, too. A storm was coming.

Davies turned abruptly and stalked back to the pagoda. The good-natured playboy in the Tommy Bahama shirt was gone. Now I finally saw the man who had the steel it would have taken to build his criminal empire. The lamb was gone. Now I faced the lion.

He pointed a finger at Emerson. "Trace that fucking account. I don't care what you have to do."

Emerson glanced at me as if he wanted me to help him

somehow. "Sir, I…"

Davies seized the side of the table in one meaty hand and flipped it over, sending it and the laptop computer crashing to the ground. "I don't give a *fuck* about the Swiss!" he shouted. "*Someone* knows where that money is going. I don't care if you have to get on a plane and fly to Zurich. Find them and get them to talk!"

Emerson put his hands in the air in a gesture of surrender. "But given the bank secrecy laws there…"

"Start cutting some balls off and we'll see about the fucking secrecy laws!" Emerson opened his mouth again but Davies was having none of it. "What the fuck are you still doing here? Go!"

Emerson shot me a terrified glance, then stood up and made a beeline for the house, scooping up the laptop as he went. I wouldn't have been entirely surprised if he was going into the house to shop for one-way plane tickets to somewhere very far away.

Davies turned to me, nostrils flaring. "And you," he said. "Do you really call yourself a fucking detective?"

I stood up and took a step toward him, getting close enough that I could smell his breath. "Choose your next words carefully," I said.

His eyes burned as he looked down at me, and I knew he was torn between threatening me and pleading with me. Finally his gaze softened. "Find my daughter," he said quietly. "Bring her back to me, and I will give you anything you want. *Anything.* Do you understand me?"

I held his gaze for a moment, then looked away,

considering my options. I could see Emerson scurrying into the house. He might well need a change of underwear once he got in there. I might have found that funny earlier, but now I actually felt sorry for the man. It was hard to imagine Davies treating employees well when he felt they'd failed him. He seemed like the kind of guy who would take a more violent approach to management.

I looked back to Davies. "I'll find your daughter," I said. "I'll find her because she's a little girl that needs help. Not because you're telling me to. I'm not afraid of you."

"Fine," he said.

I nodded at the house. "Anything he finds on that bank account, you let me know."

"As soon as I know anything, you will too."

"I'm going to go," I said. I wasn't sure what the hell I was going to do next, but I wasn't going to get anything done hanging around Davies's estate. "I'll check in soon."

"You still have my number?"

"Yeah."

He took a deep breath. "My daughter is ten years old…"

"Don't try to play that card a second time," I told him. "I said I'll find her, so I'll find her."

"I'm sorry."

"It's okay." I hesitated, not sure if I should say the rest of what was on my mind. "Look, this whole thing is fucked now. We know it and they know it. They want to get as much money from you as they can, but…"

"You think they'll kill her?"

"They're aren't going to want a witness," I said. "They want the next transfer, and maybe they think they can get another one out of you after that, but we all know this can't last forever. The clock is ticking. If you've been holding anything back, anything in reserve…"

He shook his head. "No. My cards are on the table. I understand what's at stake here."

I hoped he did. There was no guarantee that the girl was alive even now. The kidnappers could be clearing out of their hideout and heading for the border at this very moment. They could collect their last two million from anywhere in the world. The only question was whether they thought they could extend their run after that. Was it worth it to them to try and find out?

In three days we'd know for sure whether Anna was alive. I desperately wanted to find her before that. I was sure it was all the time she had.

Chapter 14

I started to drive home but pulled over at a gas station in Del Mar when I felt myself starting to shake. I spent a moment in the car with my eyes shut, palms pressed against my temples. It wasn't withdrawal. I was still too well in the bag for that. I wasn't sure how to describe what I was feeling. Stress? Panic? My skin felt like it was on too tight. If I'd been just a little bit crazier I might have taken a razor blade and tried to cut some vents in it. Just to give myself a little more space.

Do you really call yourself a fucking detective?

I had, once. I'd been good at it, too. I didn't get promoted because I was good at networking or had friends in the right places. I wasn't and I didn't. But I closed cases. I did it fast, and I never gave up. Not until the last one, anyway, when I'd finally been beaten.

My right wrist, the one the Laughing Man had broken, had started to ache. It hadn't acted up in a long time. I wonder if I'd strained it during the night, maybe stumbled during my blackout and caught it awkwardly on something. Or was it psychological? Maybe. It made very little difference. Pain was pain.

The gas station had a small market inside. I decided to go in and find something to deal with the dryness in my mouth. They didn't sell liquor, which was what I'd really gone in hoping to find, but I settled for a bag of chips and a bottle of soda. I wasn't sure how long I had been living off of junk food, but it hardly seemed worth it to waste my money on real food when I never kept anything down for long.

I sat in my car for a while and thought about my situation, eating the chips one-by-one. Why had I agreed to help Davies? It wasn't that I didn't want to find his daughter. I really did. But I knew nothing about working kidnapping cases. As much as I hated the idea of giving up, I had to admit I was the wrong person to be doing this.

But Davies had nobody else. Even if he was willing to call in the police, they might well be more interested in getting a team from their organized crime unit into his place than they would be in helping him.

I needed help. I needed another cop to talk to. Dan would be able to give me some advice if I called him. He'd be pissed at me for lying to him earlier, but at least I knew he'd talk to me once he got done yelling at me. And if he did try to get someone else from law enforcement involved, odds were they'd never get past Davies's front gate.

I'd have to deal with the yelling, I decided. But I'd never managed to find my cell phone. Had I left it in the car at some point? I checked the glove box and the storage compartment under the armrest but came up with nothing. Frustrated, I got out of the car and looked under the seats, and then in the back, running my hands into every crevice I could find. Nothing. The phone wasn't in here.

I put the car in gear and headed back to San Diego. Once I was home I was definitely going to find that phone. I'd tear my house apart if I had to. There were only so many places the damn thing could be.

But instead of looking for it, I used the house phone to call Dan's number, holding my breath as his line rang. It was time to come clean. But it was a woman's voice that answered the phone. "Who is this?" I asked. Dan wasn't senior enough in the department to have a secretary.

"It's Sarah," the voice replied. "Nevada, is that you?"

"Yeah. Hi, Sarah."

"I'm so glad you called. I was meaning to…"

"Sorry," I interrupted. I had no desire to talk about my last trip in to the station or what had happened to Todd. "Is Dan around?"

"He's out at a crime scene."

"Oh." I frowned. That was poor timing. Captains didn't go out to a lot of crime scenes, unless something political was going on, or if something very unusual had happened. "Anything I need to know about?"

"No, he's just mentoring some junior detectives," she said. "You know how he does."

"Yeah," I said. "He's that kind of guy."

"He really is."

Sometimes I thought I heard more than professional

admiration in Sarah's voice when she talked about Dan. I wondered if he had ever noticed. Probably not. Even if he had, he never would have done anything about it as long as she worked for him. It was against department regulations, and even if it hadn't been he'd have found it inappropriate. He'd wait until one of them resigned, or transferred to another division, before he made a move.

"Do you want to go out and take a look at it?" she offered. "I can give you the address. I think he'd like that."

I suppressed a chuckle. "That's okay, Sarah. I'm sure he'll be fine without me."

"I didn't mean he needed help. It's just that he cares a lot about you, and he thinks working would be a good thing for you."

They had apparently discussed this before. "Okay. Hey, Sarah?"

"Yeah?"

"Have you ever worked a kidnapping?"

"No, I never had the chance. Unless they're domestics most of those go right to the FBI."

I'd known that, of course. Most kidnappings involved children, and ever since the Lindbergh case in the 1930's, the FBI had jurisdiction over those. Police officers didn't have many opportunities to work kidnappings, at least in this country. I'd just been hoping maybe I'd get lucky with the question.

"Let me run this by you," I said. "You kidnap someone. You're holding them for ransom. Under what circumstances would you kill them?"

"None, until the ransom has been paid. You lose all your leverage if you can't come up with proof of life when you're asked for it."

Unless you had another victim, of course. Then you had at least *some* leverage. It gave them incentive to keep Anna safe, at least until they thought it was too dangerous to keep her alive anymore.

Like if Emerson was inside a possibly bugged house, making phone calls to Switzerland to try and get bank information out of someone.

Shit.

"Of course you might kill the victim by accident," Sarah offered. "Maybe during a struggle? Are we talking about any case in particular?"

"No," I said. "Thanks for your help."

"No problem."

"Hey, Sarah?"

"Hmm?"

I took a quick breath. "I was kind of rude to you the other day when I came in to the station," I said. "I'm sorry."

I heard her breathing catch. I wasn't exactly known for making apologies, even before I'd been a drunk. After a pause she said, "It's okay. Don't worry about it."

"Okay." I hadn't planned on worrying. It had just seemed like something I ought to say to her.

"Nevada? I hope you don't mind me saying so, but I was talking to a friend of mine and…" I heard her hesitate.

"Sarah?"

"My old Training Officer, you remember Paul? He runs this A.A. meeting. It's only for cops, and…"

I hung up on her.

Chapter 15

Five minutes later I called Sarah back. "When is this meeting?"

"Really?" she asked. She sounded like I'd told her I just landed on Mars and discovered it was populated by magical talking kittens who wanted to throw her a birthday party.

"When?"

"Hang on," she said. "I have to go back to my desk."

I gave her time. It wasn't like I had anything else to do.

A minute later she picked up the phone again. "Every weekday at 5:30. Weekends at 1:00."

"Where?"

"It's at the old Lutheran church on 16th Avenue. You know it? It's the one you can walk to from here."

It sounded familiar, but I figured if it was that close to police headquarters it would be easy enough to find. "So, what, you just go in the front door and they sit there in the pews?"

"No,'" she said. "You go up the main steps but there's a door on the left hand side next to the front doors that goes into a little side room. They use it for A.A. meetings and Bible study, those kinds of things."

I was curious how Sarah knew all of this but she must have anticipated the question. "Most of Paul's old trainees went with him when he got his twenty-year coin," she said. "It was a big day for him."

"Okay. 5:30?"

"That's it. Paul said you're welcome to go in and just listen…"

"That's exactly what I'm going to do," I said, hanging up on her for the second time. Listening was exactly what I needed to do right now.

If the church was where I thought it was, it was only a fifteen minute drive away. I looked at the clock. I wouldn't make it on time, but that wasn't important to me. I didn't care if I missed their opening ceremonies, or whatever it was they did there.

It turned out to be easy enough to find. I went up the steps and found the side door just as Sarah had described it. For a brief moment I considered knocking. Was that what they did? Would a slot open in the door and I'd need to say a secret password, like getting into a speakeasy during Prohibition? Then I decided I didn't actually care all that much if I broke their protocol. I opened the door and stepped inside.

The small room on the other side of the door smelled like coffee and desperation, although it's possible the desperation was just me. The room was small and square, with a dozen chairs arranged in a circle. On my right near the door sat a table with a coffee maker that held half a pot of black coffee. Someone had brought in doughnuts. Whether they were being ironic or had just wanted a snack, I didn't know.

Eight of the chairs in the circle were occupied. A heavyset man had been reading from a laminated sheet of paper as I'd entered. I only caught the words "personal inventory" before he glanced up at me and stopped abruptly. "Good *god*," he said.

I tried to place him but couldn't. I'd had enough notoriety on the force that most cops recognized me immediately, but I never socialized all that much. I'd been something of a recluse even before I'd started drinking.

A few of the others I recognized. Mike Brown had been a detective in Robbery but had been busted down to patrolman for, believe it or not, drinking on the job. Jason London worked Narcotics. He was in his mid-forties but looked older, substance abuse having done a number on his skin. Not all of the Narcotics guys got out clean.

Three of the cops were in uniform. I didn't recognize any of them. Too young.

An older man with a neatly trimmed white beard stood up. I recognized him as Sarah's Training Officer but I wasn't sure we'd ever actually met. Paul…Wilson? Wilkins? Something like that.

"Nevada," Paul said. He had a grandfatherly tone that a lot of people probably found comforting, but it just made me want to punch him in the face. "Come in. Have a seat." He motioned to one of the empty chairs.

"I'm fine," I said.

Paul smiled gently. "This is a safe place, Nevada. You're with friends here."

"I don't have time for this," I said. I held my hand up like I was a student in class and wanted to ask a question. "Hi, I'm Nevada, and I'm an alcoholic."

"Hi, Nevada," two of the cops responded automatically. The rest just stared at me.

"So we've established that," I said. "Great. Good job, everyone. I'll say a bunch of Hail Marys later. Right now, I've got a case I need help with."

Paul took a step forward, raising both hands patiently. "We don't talk about the job here, Nevada, except for as to how it affects our sobriety. We're here to support each other with our disease."

"You know what?" I asked. "That's great. I support that. I really do."

"Okay, then…" he glanced at the empty chair meaningfully, then back at me.

"But I've got a little girl out there who is going to die if I don't find her," I continued. "I mean, she is literally going to die, and very soon. Right now I need a room full of cops more than anything else. So, let's take a vote." I turned to the assembled drunks. "Who wants to talk about the twelve steps, and who wants to help me save a child's life? Everyone for working the steps, raise their hand."

Nobody raised their hand. I nodded. "Okay, it's no votes for doing the steps. Now, everyone who wants to save a little girl?" I put my hand up. Nobody else did. Two of the patrol cops exchanged a confused glance.

"What the fuck?" I asked. "Am I speaking goddamn Chinese here?"

Jason London raised his hand slowly. I pointed at him. "Right there! We have a winner!"

Jason gave Paul a plaintive look. "Maybe we could hear her out?"

"I'm not sure we have a choice," Paul said. He went back to his chair and sat down. "Why don't you take a seat, Nevada, and you can tell us what's going on."

I sat. For the next fifteen minutes I laid out everything I knew about the case, from the moment Chandler Emerson had arrived at my doorstep until the moment I'd crashed Paul's A.A. meeting for help. "Sorry about that," I added, nodding at Paul.

"You were never known for doing anything the conventional way," Paul acknowledged. "I used to wonder if that was why you had so much success as a detective."

"And why you fell so far," said Jason London.

I gave Jason a look that suggested I'd like to see him fall from a great height. After a moment he looked away. Nobody ever won a staring contest with me. People didn't like what they saw in my eyes.

"It's weird for a kidnapping," one of the plainclothes cops said.

I snapped my fingers and pointed at her. "You are?"

"Miranda Callies." I cocked my head at her. I'd never heard her name before. "Gang unit."

"Why is it weird, Miranda?"

"You said the men on the phone were Mexicans?"

"It's a guess from the accent. They spoke Spanish. I'm no expert; they honestly could have been from anywhere."

"I heard kidnappings are pretty common in Latin America," one of the patrol cops said. Everyone looked at him and he shrugged. "Fine, I saw it on National Geographic."

"They *are* common," Miranda said. "They're damn near endemic in some areas. It's the target that's weird."

"Davies is rich," I told her. "I saw him transfer two million dollars out of his bank account without breaking a sweat, and it wasn't the first payment he'd made."

"Lots of people are rich," Miranda said. "But lots of people aren't going to send a small army of killers after you once you've collected your ransom."

"Davies will go to war," said Jason London.

"And it's not just about the money," Miranda continued. "He *has* to kill them just to keep his reputation intact. Whoever did this, Davies is never going to stop looking for them. And when he catches up to them he'll skin them alive and FedEx what's left of them to their families. Then he'll kill their families."

"You would have to be suicidal to take him on," said Paul.

"What if you were bigger and stronger?" asked one of the patrol cops.

"It still wouldn't be worth a war," Miranda said. "It'd be much easier to go find a rich businessman and kidnap him. Then you ransom him to his family. In some places they even sell insurance for that kind of thing. Do it in certain countries and you won't even need to worry about the police if you cut the right guy in for a share. There are lots of easier ways to get that much money."

I nodded. I'd definitely had the right idea in coming here. Working with a roomful of cops was giving me insight I'd lacked before, and if helping me wasn't the reason they'd come here today, there were worse ways they could be spending their time.

"How did they get into the condo in the first place?" Paul asked.

I looked at him and frowned. I'd pondered that question as well. "What do you mean?"

He scratched his beard thoughtfully. "You said someone took two furniture crates into the building, stuffed the woman and her daughter inside, and then took them out of the building that way."

"Yeah. I figured she would have opened the door to tell them to leave and the kidnappers must have forced their way inside."

"But that doesn't work," Paul said. "It's one thing to walk up to your house with a box and knock on the door, but the Davies woman lived in a secure building."

The guard would never have let them past, I thought. He'd have called up to check it with Heather and she'd have told him right away she wasn't getting any furniture delivered. The guard should have turned the kidnappers away while they'd still been in the lobby.

So how did the kidnappers make it to her door in the first

place? Had someone paid off the security guard? That was an interesting thought. If so, it meant there was someone else I could question.

I stood up. "I have to go," I said. "You guys have been great. I mean, for a bunch of drunks." I frowned. "You know, that came out wrong. Seriously, thank you."

Paul stood up. "I guess there's no point in asking you to stay," he said. "We meet here every weekday at 5:30 for an hour. If you want to come back…"

"Probably not."

He went into his wallet and pulled out a business card. "Take this, at least. My number is on there." He handed it to me.

I looked at the card. It had his first name, a telephone number, and, "This says you're a friend of Bill W."

"That's right."

"Which one of you is Bill W.?"

He smiled gently. "Come back sometime and I'll tell you about him."

His voice had the same tone Christians use when they say they want to tell you about Jesus. I shrugged, intending to flip the card into the garbage as soon as I stepped outside, but instead I tucked it into my back pocket. "I do appreciate the help," I said.

"Tell us how it works out," one of the patrol cops said.

"And good luck," Mike Brown added.

"Thanks," I said. Odds were I was going to need it.

Chapter 16

I felt my legs starting to tremble as I walked back to my Mustang. When was the last time I'd had a drink? This morning? Yes, and I'd thrown that up. That might be a new record for my sobriety, although to be fair I'd still been pretty drunk when I'd woken up this morning.

Withdrawal wasn't on the agenda tonight. I needed to get a drink soon if I was going to stay functional. When this was all over I really needed to think about seeing a doctor, maybe get some tests done and see what was going on with my liver. If I even still had a liver. Experience told me I would never actually make the appointment, but at least I could pretend to think about it.

I drove three blocks up the street until I came to a run-down liquor store, the kind with steel bars over the windows that were ubiquitous in bad neighborhoods. Inside I picked up an energy drink and a flask-sized bottle of cheap vodka. The cashier stuck it in a paper bag for me, the camouflage of street alcoholics everywhere. I didn't need it. I had a car to drink it in.

Once I got back behind the wheel I choked down three large mouthfuls of vodka, nearly vomiting after the third. I had to swallow hard a good dozen times afterward to suppress my gag reflex. It was hard not to notice that the act of drinking itself had been getting more difficult lately. I was probably so poisoned by this point that my body couldn't stand taking any more alcohol in. My body would have to deal. I didn't have time to have a seizure today.

When I was sure I could keep the alcohol down I raised my right hand into the air and watched it for a moment. It was pretty far from steady, but once the liquor took hold I should be fine for a while. At least for long enough for me to get up to Heather's condo and ask some questions.

I considered taking the rest of the vodka along with me, but decided instead to get rid of it. There was no need to have an open container in the car if I did get stopped. I was about to chuck the bottle into the trash can outside the store when I spotted a homeless guy snoring on the sidewalk half a block away. I walked over and sat the paper bag down next to him. He needed it more than the trash can did.

Back in the car I took a long look at myself in the visor mirror. I really did look like someone who had been dead for a while. I didn't like it all that much. I'd never been beautiful, but I'd certainly looked a hell of a lot better than *this*.

For one brief moment I thought about driving the three blocks back to the A.A. meeting and sitting there for the rest of the hour. It wouldn't take long. But I needed to work. Time was too important now, and what good was sitting in a church possibly going to do me? I could find out who Bill W. was some other time.

I put the car in gear and squealed the tires as I pulled away from the curb, starting off for Heather Davies's condo in La Jolla.

The security guard in the lobby was the same guy I'd talked to when I'd been here the other night, meaning he wasn't the guy who had been here when Heather's kidnappers had taken her away. I'd never bothered to get the guy's name. He looked up at me as I entered the lobby. Recognition showed on his face, but I could also see a question written there.

"Hi there," I smiled.

"Hello," he replied.

"Nice night tonight?"

"It's…fine," he said. "Ms…"

"James."

"That's right," he said, the question on his face answered now. "It's Nevada, isn't it?"

"It is. What's your name?"

"Jack."

"Jack…"

"Jack Stevens."

I watched him for a moment, hoping I had enough intuition left to let me know if he was hiding something from me. "You know, Jack, you knew me right away the last time I was here. You said, 'Good evening, Ms. James.'"

"I'm sorry about that," he said. "I'd been told to expect you just before you arrived."

Truth, I thought. "That's how it works in a place like this, isn't it?"

"How's that?"

"Let's do an experiment. I walk in here and say, 'Hi, I'm Nevada James. I'm here to visit Bill Jones in unit 112.'"

He frowned. "But there isn't a Bill Jones in unit 112. That's Mr. Anderson."

"It's an experiment, Jack. Work with me here. What would you say?"

Jack clearly wasn't used to this kind of bold thinking. "I'd say that I need to call up to Mr. Anderson...uh, Mr. Jones...and let him know you're here."

"Oh, but we're old friends, Bill and I. I just got in from Tallahassee and I want to surprise him."

"Tallahassee?"

"It's just an example."

"I still need to call him," Jack said. "It's the rules."

"That's what I thought," I said. "What if Bill had told you in advance he was expecting me and to just let me go on past?"

"I'd let you go on past."

"You wouldn't call up?"

"Not necessarily, no. Maybe." He looked like he'd just bet everything on the last *Jeopardy!* question and couldn't decide between two answers.

"Close enough," I said "Same with deliveries?"

"Ma'am?"

"I've got flowers for Bill Jones. Can I go on up to 112 or

are you going to call him?"

"You don't have any…" he started to say. "Yes, I'm going to have to call up."

"Now, instead of flowers, I've got two enormous crates."

"What's in the crates?"

"Does it really matter what's in the crates?"

He thought about it. "I guess not."

"Okay. Are you calling up to Bill?"

"Of course."

"Unless?"

He thought about it. "Unless I knew the crates were coming and had been told to send them up."

"We're getting somewhere now," I said. "The last delivery Heather Davies received was two crates. It's on your list, in the drawer there."

He retrieved his clipboard from the desk drawer and started flipping through it. "In at 2:53," I remembered.

"Out at 3:20," he nodded. "You're right."

"I know you guys didn't call up to Heather Davies," I said. "But she wasn't expecting any delivery. She never told you to let anyone go by."

"Oh."

"So who told you guys the crates were coming?"

He looked at his clipboard. "Nobody."

"Nobody?"

"There was no need," Jack said. "He signed the crates in himself."

That wasn't what I had been expecting. "Who signed them in?"

Jack turned the clipboard around and showed it to me. Next to the in and out times was a signature block. I'd never seen his signature before, but it was there, as prim, proper, and somehow as arrogant as I would have expected it to be: Chandler Emerson.

Chapter 17

"Well, I'll be goddamned," I said.

"Ma'am?"

I didn't answer him. I was busy trying to work out whether I was the world's biggest idiot. It was starting to look that way.

"Is everything all right?" Jack asked.

"Not really," I said. The signature could have been forged, of course. If they didn't have one on file to compare it to, how would the guards have ever known? I could have done it myself if I'd wanted to, although I might have been tempted to replace the "s" in Emerson's name with a dollar sign.

"Do you…want me to call someone?"

"How do you know Chandler Emerson signed that?" I asked, pointing at the signature. "Couldn't anyone walk in here and sign his name there?"

"No," Jack said. "We check IDs, but in his case the guard on duty probably knew him by sight and didn't need to. Mr.

Emerson is on the lease. He's been here before, plenty of times."

I'd seen Emerson's name on the lease when I'd been going through Heather's paperwork. It made sense that any of the guards here might have seen him before.

"I've met him myself once or twice," Jack said, as if he had just read my mind.

"How nice for you," I murmured. Emerson was definitely involved. But was he behind it or was he just a pawn, like poor Todd had been? I'd read him as a small, scared man, not someone who had the steel to pull something like this off. Could I have been *that* wrong?

God, I really needed to quit drinking.

"Do you want me to call Mr. Emerson?" Jack asked. His hand had strayed toward the desk drawer. "I have his number in here somewhere."

"No," I said. "No need. I'm going to see him later on." That was probably true. Chances were I'd be seeing Emerson again *very* soon. Unless he was on a plane out of the country, which was exactly where I'd be right now if I were him.

I left Jack in the lobby and went to sit in my car, wishing I hadn't given my vodka to that homeless guy earlier. Maybe I could go and get it back from him. Or I could just buy more. That sounded like a much better idea.

Once again I found myself wishing I had my cell phone handy. I really needed to track that damn thing down. Or maybe I'd just pick up a burner the next time I was in a convenience store. Pay phones were a thing of the past these days; you hardly ever saw them and who carried that many quarters, anyway? I couldn't be running home every time I needed to make a phone call.

It was getting late. Dan had been out at a crime scene earlier, which meant there was a good chance he was still in the office doing paperwork and brooding. I could stop by and pick his brain. I could even tell him I'd gone to an A.A. meeting, which might get me back onto his good side after I'd told him I'd lied to him when I'd told him I thought I was working on nothing more interesting than a domestic dispute.

But what I really wanted right now was information, and it was the kind that Dan wouldn't be able to give me without getting a warrant. And given that he was a homicide detective with no jurisdiction over a kidnapping case that should have gone straight to the FBI anyway, that warrant was never going to come.

There were other ways to get information, though.

I put the car in gear and headed for Santee, a small suburban city just northeast of San Diego. I hadn't been out there in years. Santee wasn't on the way to anything and there was no real reason to go there unless you called it home. But I had someone I wanted to see and I was fairly sure I could still find his house, unless he had moved. In that case, I'd be screwed.

There had been road construction on the way to Santee and the freeway didn't run the way I remembered it. I wound up taking the wrong exit off of Route 52, but eventually found the McMansion I was looking for in a relatively upscale neighborhood. It was certainly nicer than *my* neighborhood, anyway, but after spending so much time at Alan Davies's estate I was beginning to take a second look at anything, assuming people were broke if they didn't have columns and marble fountains in front of their houses.

I got out of the car and went to ring the doorbell. After a brief moment an impossibly handsome man answered the door. He wore tight blue jeans, no shirt, and had silky brown hair that reached down to his shoulders. He looked like he'd stepped out of a Calvin Klein catalog.

"Wow," I said.

He smiled at me. "Can I help you, miss?"

Miss? He was my new favorite person in the world. I opened my mouth to speak but realized I'd forgotten what I'd come here for. I'd also forgotten most of the words in the English language. I managed to make a strange squeaking noise before I shut my mouth again.

"Who is it?" a new voice asked. The shirtless Adonis stepped aside and I saw the man I'd been looking for. Scott Landers was in his mid-forties, lean with a swimmer's build, and wore small circular eyeglasses that made him look like John Lennon with a Wall Street haircut. "Good god!" he said, his face turning white. "Nevada!"

"Scott," I said, trying to get my thoughts together before I made a fool of myself.

"Is this…" he began. "My, god. You caught him?"

My heart sank. I should have called Scott before I showed up on his doorstep. He thought I'd come to give him the news he'd been waiting so long to hear in person. That I'd caught the Laughing Man. Or better yet, that I'd killed him slowly.

I needed to find my goddamn cell phone.

"No," I said, shaking my head. "I'm sorry. It's not about that."

He sighed. "I wouldn't have been that lucky, I guess. Well, come in. It's nice to see you. Quite a surprise, but nice."

Scott showed me inside. I'd been here before several times in the past, but it had been quite a while and he'd remodeled the interior since then, probably spending more on his living room than I'd made in the best year of my life. We sat down on leather couches while the Mayor of Hot Town took his shirtless self into the kitchen to make tea.

"New boyfriend?" I asked Scott.

"Fiancée, now," he said. "But I doubt you came to RSVP in person." He noted my confused look. "I sent you a wedding invitation some time ago."

I'd never noticed it. It had probably gone into the trash with a pile of unpaid bills. "Congratulations," I said. "He's...he's really something."

"He is, isn't he?" Scott smiled, but his eyes betrayed his disappointment in me. "Jean-Paul owns a salon in the Gaslamp. You really should let him take a look at your hair. It looks like you've been cutting it yourself."

"When it gets in my eyes," I admitted. I'd been taking kitchen shears to it every now and then for at least a few years.

Jean-Paul returned to the living room with a steaming teapot and three cups on a tray that he placed carefully on the glass coffee table between us. He reached out and took a lock of my hair in his fingers, feeling it between them for a moment. Any other man who tried that would have gotten a broken arm for his trouble, but I decided Jean-Paul could do anything he wanted.

"I love a challenge," Jean-Paul told me. "Come see me next week. I'll give you one of my cards before you go."

I wanted to say yes but was afraid I'd just make another squeaking sound, so I kept my mouth shut.

Jean-Paul took a seat next to Scott. "I suspect this isn't a social call," Scott said.

"No," I admitted, a bit ashamed of myself. Scott deserved better than this. He'd spent years waiting for me to come to him with good news, but all I had was a request that he do something very illegal for me.

"Have you come for financial advice? Why do I doubt that?"

"Because you know I don't have any money to invest."

"Then…"

I glanced at Jean-Paul, then back at Scott, trying to ask a question without saying it out loud.

"Jean-Paul knows about my past," Scott said.

"We share everything," Jean-Paul confirmed.

I nodded. That would make this a lot less awkward. Scott Landers was a stockbroker and had made a small fortune in the early 2000's investing in tech stocks. What was less known was that prior to his career in finance, he had been one of the most notorious computer hackers on the West Coast. He'd made a large fortune by cracking bank systems and making money vanish from accounts, only to reappear in accounts he controlled. I had no idea how much he'd gotten away with before he retired. Nor did the FBI, who was still looking for

"The Red Mockingbird," the only name they'd ever known him by. I imagined the NSA and half a dozen other government agencies would also have liked to know his current whereabouts.

I broke down the case for Scott. He listened patiently, absently toying with Jean-Paul's hair while I talked. I wondered if they'd mind if I toyed with Jean-Paul's hair, also. He'd touched mine, after all. It only seemed fair.

Scott was quiet for a moment after I'd finished, sipping his tea. "It sounds to me like you need information, but that this information would be difficult for you to come by through legitimate means."

"Everything there is to know about Emerson's money," I nodded. "If he's getting payments that can't be accounted for. If he's spending money that can't be accounted for. Where he shops, if he just bought a million dollars in Swiss bearer bonds, a house in Antigua, or a case of gold coins…" I frowned, something just having occurred to me. "If I got you the account number of the Swiss bank could you…"

"No," he cut me off. "Not in the time frame you need it by, anyway. The Swiss may be the only people in the world who do security right."

"But Emerson's accounts?"

"Anything in the U.S. I can get you a pretty good look at."

"How long?"

"Not long, but I have to put some equipment together and then I'll have to take it…somewhere else."

I nodded. "Could the FBI track it back to you here?"

"Not yet," Scott said. "But in ten years, who knows what they'll be able to do? So it won't be done from here."

"There's a reason you never got caught," I said. Scott was one of the most careful people I knew.

"I know," he nodded. "Tomorrow afternoon, maybe. I realize time is not on your side, but that's the best I can do. I have to be careful about this."

"Okay. Thanks." I knew not to push him.

He looked at me coldly. "It's not free, Nevada."

"I don't have anything now. Davies will pay me when I have his daughter."

Scott sighed and rolled his eyes. "Good god. Do you really think I'm talking about money?" He turned to Jean-Paul. "Dear, Nevada looks like she's been washing her hair with something she found growing under her sink. Do you think you could put together a little care package for her?"

Jean-Paul and I both knew that was a pathetic excuse to get him out of the room for a few minutes. He smiled gently at Scott and left us alone.

Scott waited until he was sure Jean-Paul was gone, and then his calm expression melted away into one of long-suppressed anger. "I went to an A.A. meeting…" I began.

"Oh, shut up," he snapped. I shut up and let him glare at me, my hands folded in my lap. I'd known this was coming when I'd seen him at the door.

Scott's eyes were on fire. "My brother is rotting in the ground," he finally said. "He is *in the ground*. Do you know what next week is?"

Was he kidding? Half the time I didn't know what *year* it was. But he wouldn't have asked unless… "His birthday."

"His birthday," Scott said. "So next week I'll drive my mother out to his grave. She'll put flowers next to his headstone and cry, and I'll cry, and you know what, Nevada? I would like to tell her that we can take some small comfort in the fact that his killer was brought to justice. And it would only be a small comfort, but it would be *something*, at least. But I can't do that this year. *Again*."

"No," I said quietly.

"Do you know why?"

"Of course I know why."

I knew he was going to tell me anyway. "Because the only person actually capable of *catching* the Laughing Man is too busy drinking herself to death in her shitty little house. Hmm? Because Nevada James would rather feel sorry for herself than *get off her ass* and go do something about it."

Those were fighting words, but I had nothing to fight with. He wasn't wrong. "It's a nice house," I protested weakly.

"It *was* a nice house before you trashed it." I looked up at him, surprised that he knew that. "I know what your house looks like, Nevada. I went to see you three months ago."

"You did?"

"I did. I'm a very proud man, but I was prepared to get on my knees and beg you for help. I had reached the point where I was willing to beg. Do you know what that's like? To beg for help?"

"I wasn't home, I guess." I *hoped*.

"You *were* home. You were drunk and incoherent. I don't think you even knew who I was."

I shook my head. That wasn't what I'd wanted to hear. "I'm sorry. I don't remember that."

"I'm not surprised."

"Look, I've had a rough time…"

"Oh, *fuck* your rough time. I am so sick of hearing about your rough time. *Everyone* has had a rough time, Nevada. Either get over it or kill yourself."

I couldn't look directly at him. The carpet was much less judgmental. I looked at it instead.

"You know what, Nevada? He beat you. Fine. He beat you and I know he hurt you very badly. I don't blame you for losing it for a while. God knows I probably would have, too, if I'd been in your place." He leaned forward. "You know what's great about people, sweetheart? We get better. We get sick, and then we get better. It's time for you to get back on your feet."

I could feel Jean-Paul hovering just beyond the entryway to the next room, waiting until Scott finished with me before he came in. It was sweet of him to let me have that little bit of dignity.

"I'm trying," I said to Scott.

"*Try harder.*"

"Okay."

"Okay." He sighed. "Jean-Paul? We're done."

Jean-Paul came back into the living room, carrying a small wicker basket filled with bottles. "For you, dear," he said gently. I looked inside and saw he'd assembled a collection of shampoos and conditioners, a few bars of soap, and other things I didn't recognize. I'd never been much of a girly-girl. "Give me a call," Jean-Paul said, stroking my hair again. "I could do wonders with this."

"Thanks," I said quietly. I didn't want to look at him, or at anyone else, ever again.

Jean-Paul sat down next to Scott and squeezed his hand. Scott smiled weakly at him. I could see his eyes were wet. It seemed like I made every man that knew me cry these days.

"You'll call me?" I asked Scott.

"Of course not," he snapped. "You'll be contacted."

In a way that could never be traced back to him, no doubt. I stood up. "Thanks for seeing me."

He looked up at me. "I meant what I said. Do we understand each other?"

"Getting back on my feet," I said. "You got it." But I didn't believe it, and I knew he didn't, either.

Chapter 18

Back in my car, I put my hands on the steering wheel and cried for a good five minutes.

The disappointment and anger Scott had expressed in me had been too much to take. And the worst part of it was that he was right. I had failed. The Laughing Man had knocked me down and I hadn't gotten back up. I'd surrendered. I'd spent the last three years destroying myself, finishing the job he had started for him. How many times had I wished he'd killed me? He could have done it easily enough. It would have been so simple for him to cut me up and pose me in the still-life he had created out of what was left of those two little girls I'd been trying to save.

But it had been a game to him. Like checkers, or maybe chess, and a chess game didn't usually end with the winner murdering the loser. He'd wanted to savor his victory, and he'd wanted me to be alive while he did it. He'd wanted me to live with the knowledge that he'd won our game.

God, I needed a drink.

I drove home, stopping at a liquor store along the way for two bottles of vodka and a packaged ham sandwich. I opened one of the bottles in my car and took a long drink out of it, then stashed them under the passenger seat for the drive home.

The ham sandwich was awful, but I needed food. I ate it as I drove, flinging the stale crusts out the window onto the freeway. If someone wanted to report me for throwing bread at them, they could go ahead and do it. Good luck finding the evidence later.

Back home I poured a tumbler full of vodka and downed half of it. Then I went to find the business card Davies had given me. Once I had it in hand I dialed his number from the house phone.

He answered on the second ring. "You have her?"

One more person I was about to disappoint tonight. "No," I said. "I was wondering if Chandler had found anything on that Swiss bank account."

"Chandler is on his way to Switzerland right now."

I blinked. "Really?"

"He took two of my best people and got on a plane. I told him I don't care what he has to do as long as he gets me some answers."

"Okay," I said. That wasn't what I'd been expecting. I'd thought if I could get Emerson on the phone I could trick some information out of him, maybe even get an idea of who he was working for. But if he was flying to Switzerland, well, he sure as hell didn't have Anna with him.

"Are you making any progress?" Davies asked.

"Not yet," I said, "but I'm working on a lead."

"What is it?"

"Just trying to figure out who would be fool enough to kidnap your family," I said. "It's not a smart play for a lot of reasons." I didn't think he needed to know I hadn't worked that out until I'd gone to an A.A. meeting.

"No," he said. "Someone is going to die for this."

"Maybe you don't want to tell me that."

"I guess not," he said. "Well, keep at it. I meant what I said before. Give me my daughter and I'll give you anything you want."

The truth was I wanted a lot of things, but the only one he could really provide me with was money. That would have to be good enough.

I said good night and hung up the phone. I could have told him Emerson was somehow involved, of course, but if he reacted by pulling the lawyer's head off, it was a death sentence for his daughter. I had a better chance of keeping her alive if I kept quiet for now. It was too early in the game to show all of my cards.

Game?

It was getting late but I wasn't tired. I seemed to be getting more manic, and the vodka wasn't shutting me down the way it usually did. I switched on the television, remembered I hadn't paid my cable bill, and shut it off. I needed something to do.

Of course. I would finally find my cell phone.

Half an hour later I had not found my cell phone. After looking in every drawer and cabinet in the house I'd found nothing but dirty laundry and garbage. A search under my couch cushions yielded nothing more but some loose change, horrifically decomposed food, and a motorcycle magazine I'd bought two years ago.

In the kitchen I dispensed with the glass and took a long drink of vodka directly from the open bottle. I could feel the heat of the alcohol finally spreading throughout my body, down my arms and legs, and my head had the familiar fuzziness I'd been craving. That was it. Now I'd be able to sleep tonight.

I sat back down on my couch and watched the blank television screen for a while. The vodka was rapidly overtaking my brain now, coming on like a tidal wave. I'd had too much of it too fast, but I didn't care. Pretty soon I'd be...

Chapter 19

The sun was just starting to go down when I came to. I blinked once against the sunlight coming in through the window and thought about that. It had been late at night when I'd gotten home and started drinking. Or continued drinking, anyway. How long had I been out?

I'd changed clothes in the interim. I didn't remember that. I'd been in a blackout, then. I'd been up and active, but the part of my brain that recorded memories had been turned off. It was a much more dangerous state than just drinking too much and passing out. Asleep I'd have been harmless. Awake and without the ability to form memories? Who knew what I'd done?

My mouth was dry. I went into the kitchen to pour myself a drink. I was surprised to find a third bottle on the counter that hadn't been there the night before. That was a bad sign. It meant I'd been out of the house. It wasn't unusual for me to buy more alcohol during a blackout, but it also meant there were plenty of things that could have gone wrong on the way to the store and back.

My front door was closed and locked. So at least I'd done that much right.

I looked out the window to the street, expecting to see my car parked there. It wasn't. Uh-oh.

I stepped outside and looked up and down the street. The car was nowhere in view. I finally spotted it when I turned around and saw it parked in my open garage. Something didn't look quite right, though. I got closer and saw that at some point I'd driven the car into the back wall of the garage. There didn't appear to be much damage, but the impact had been enough to set off the car's airbags. I wasn't going to be driving it for a while.

The keys were still in the ignition. I took them out and stuck them in my pocket, cursing my own stupidity as I did so. I needed the damn car. Why had I gotten so drunk last night? Because Scott had called me out on my own bullshit? That had to be the worst excuse of all time.

I ran my fingers through my hair and my hands came out covered with what looked like chalk. It must have been left there when the airbags went off. That was probably why I'd changed my clothes, but I hadn't bothered to shower. I'd get around to that.

I hit the switch to close the garage door and went back into the house. Back in the kitchen I poured half an inch of vodka into a glass and sipped it slowly, then put the bottle I'd obtained during the blackout away. This was a sign I needed to take it easy on the stuff, obviously. I was going to have to call a damn tow truck to get the car to the shop, and new airbags would be expensive. It was good thing I had a rich gangster client.

Good god. Was this really what my life had come to?

The wind chimes rang and this time I remembered immediately that that was the sound of my doorbell. Had someone come to check on me? I started for the door, but my body started shaking and my legs went out from under me halfway there. I fell to the ground and retched once, then leaned forward and vomited on the carpet, unable to control myself.

I wasn't surprised to see there was no food in what came up. I was surprised by the amount of yellow liquid, given that I drank vodka almost exclusively. Had I gotten my hands on tequila at some point? Or was that...*bile?* Jesus *fucking* Christ. When this was over I'd definitely have to think about seeing a doctor. I knew I'd never go through with it, but maybe if I thought about it *really hard* it would help.

My shaking didn't seem to be subsiding but it wasn't bad enough that I couldn't get to the door. Hopefully it would be Scott with the information I needed. If Dan or Sarah saw me in this condition I was going to have to talk my way out of a trip to the hospital.

When I opened the door I was surprised to see a handsome young man standing there with a messenger bag. He didn't have the beauty Jean-Paul had dazzled me with, but I could have believed he'd also stepped off the pages of a catalog, although something a little more budget. Behind him another equally handsome young man was waiting next to a red convertible.

"Are you Abercrombie or Fitch?" I asked, crossing my arms in front of me. I suddenly had the chills, even though it was a warm night.

"Good evening," he said, ignoring my clever quip.

"Good evening." I squinted at the receding sun. "What time is it?"

He nodded understandingly. "Scott said you might be needing this." He took a brown paper sack out of the messenger bag and handed it to me.

"What is this?" I asked. "Booze?" Had Scott known I'd need some maintenance?

"Vitamins," the young man replied.

I opened the bag and peered inside. It held several bottles that looked like they'd come from GNC. There was a multivitamin and separate bottles of B-complex, D-3, and milk thistle. The last one was an herb I recognized. It was supposed to be good for your liver.

"Oh," I said. "Tell him I said thanks."

"He said you can shove your thanks up your ass, take the goddamn vitamins."

I blinked. "Is he…" I looked around. "Is he *listening* right now?"

"No. He anticipated what you'd say. He also had a response for the Abercrombie & Fitch joke he knew you'd make, but I didn't think it was worth repeating."

"Oh. Okay. Thanks."

"You're welcome."

"Do you have a name?"

"No," the young man said. He knelt down and removed a

thin laptop computer from the messenger bag, along with its power supply. He carefully put the power supply on top of the laptop and handed them both to me.

I took them. "I already have a computer."

"Your computer is shit."

"Okay. He told you to say that?"

"He did, but I probably would have said it anyway. Compared to that one, most computers are shit."

"Great," I said. "Well, you're fun."

The young man ignored me and removed a flash drive from the messenger bag. He held it up for me to see. "This contains the information you're looking for."

I reached for it but he pulled it away. "Wait," he said. "This drive contains a virus that will cause it to self-destruct two hours after the first time you plug it in. It will do this whether it is plugged in at the time or not. It doesn't matter."

"What, it's going to explode?"

He looked at me like I'd asked if it was going to turn into a pumpkin. "Of course not. It will irreversibly encrypt and then corrupt itself."

"Okay. Good to know."

"Yes, it is. Two hours is more time than you need, but it is important that you be...fully awake...when you begin."

"He told you to say *sober*, didn't he?"

The young man nodded. "I assumed you would take my meaning."

"I did."

"When it is finished you should smash the drive with a hammer and dispose of its pieces in at least four different locations, none of which should be within a mile of here, or each other."

"Now you're just fucking with me," I said. He stared back at me impassively. "Okay, I guess you're not. Got it. Anything else?"

"Don't forget to take the vitamins. And, good luck." With that, the young man picked up his bag, nodded once at me, and started back down my walk. When he reached the other young man they kissed once, then got in the convertible and drove away together, perhaps heading off to play beach volleyball or cuddle puppies. Whatever it was Abercrombie & Fitch models did on their days off.

I took the computer back inside and sat it down on my dining room table. I'd have time for that in a minute. A more pressing concern was the mess I'd just made in the living room. I found a clean dishtowel in the kitchen and laid it out over the spot where I'd vomited on the carpet. I didn't have the energy to clean it up, and the smell would likely make me vomit again. I was content to let it dry for now.

Back in the kitchen I went through the vitamins and took one of each, washing them down with a good swallow of vodka. That should take care of any vitamin deficiency I might have had and my shaking in one move. The vodka nearly made me gag but I kept it down. I couldn't afford to overdo it. I had work to do, and I'd wasted too much time already. Most of this day had been lost because I'd been in a blackout. On the other hand, I'd probably be up all night tonight, so I had plenty of time to work.

The laptop Scott had sent over booted to its home screen much faster than I'd ever seen a computer do before. I didn't recognize the operating system but it was something similar enough to the way a Macintosh worked that using it was fairly intuitive. He'd been right. Compared to this, my computer *was* shit.

I hesitated just a moment, then plugged the flash drive into the side of the computer. Two hours. That should be plenty of time.

Two clicks brought up the drive's contents, which consisted of one PDF file. I clicked it open and found myself looking at a copy of Chandler Emerson's driver's license. It didn't look like someone had taken the license and run off a copy on a Xerox machine. This appeared to have come directly from the DMV's own system. Well, that wasn't really a surprise. Scott could probably hack the DMV with an old calculator, if he really wanted to.

The next page was a full copy of Emerson's passport. He got around. He been to Thailand, Hong Kong, Grand Cayman, Saint Kitts and Nevis, and all over Europe. I didn't see Switzerland among his passport stamps, but that wasn't enough to vindicate him as far as I was concerned. If he owned the Swiss account that Davies's money was going to, he wouldn't necessarily have needed to go there personally to open it.

Next up were his tax returns. Davies Holdings was listed as his only employer. I was a bit startled at the amount of money he was making as a mob lawyer. He'd pulled in more last year than I'd made in my entire career as a cop.

Emerson's credit report was next. My jaw dropped when I

saw his credit score. I hadn't known the numbers went up that high.

The credit report was followed by six months' worth of bank statements. I sipped my vodka as I looked at what he spent his money on. There were plenty of restaurant charges, and none from grocery stores. He didn't do a lot of cooking at home, then. He had a Netflix subscription. I'd had one, once, back before I'd stopped paying them.

There was nothing odd in his deposits. He received one lump sum every month from Davies Holdings. I couldn't find a single incoming transfer from any other location. He wasn't getting money sent to this account from any Swiss banks, or any other place as far as I could see.

I went through the bank statements a second time, sure I must have missed something. And I had, although it took me a moment to notice what it was. Emerson had a sizeable mortgage payment he made every month, but beginning three months ago he had begun making a second mortgage payment to a different bank in Oceanside, a coastal city forty-five minutes north of here.

That didn't make any sense. There was no way Emerson was planning to move to Oceanside. It was a nice enough city, but way too blue-collar for someone with his means and overinflated sense of self-importance. He'd consider it beneath him, something akin to moving into a homeless shelter.

I flipped through the PDF and found his first mortgage statement. The address given was on an expensive street in La Jolla. That would be his primary residence, then. That made sense.

The second mortgage statement was also in the file.

Someone had circled the address in black pen and written "REALLY?" next to it in capital letters before scanning it into the file. So Scott had noticed the oddity as well. He must have expected I'd have been pretty drunk if he'd thought I'd miss that. Well, I'd shown him. I was only slightly drunk and I hadn't missed it.

I wrote down the address of the second house and looked through the rest of the PDF, but there was nothing else I could use in there. Scott had only had a day to come up with this, after all. And he'd given me something interesting. There were plenty of reasons a wealthy man might want to have a second house somewhere out of the way. To keep a mistress, for example. It wasn't unheard of, for people of sufficient means.

But a second house nobody else knew about would also be a great place to hide a kidnapping victim. I was willing to put money on Anna being in that house.

I drained my glass, feeling the vodka warm in my stomach. I didn't fill a second glass. I had enough alcohol in me to keep me functional for a while, but hopefully not enough that I was in danger of falling asleep. Besides, right now I needed to be able to keep my balance. It was time to go to Oceanside, and I was pretty sure there was only one way I'd be able to do it.

Chapter 20

I didn't have a printer at home, but after a few minutes of looking at maps on Google I was pretty sure I could find Emerson's second house without too much trouble. If it turned out to be a problem I could always stop and buy a map at a gas station.

It occurred to me that I ought to call Dan Evans, or Sarah, or even Davies before I left. But as soon as I did that, I'd be taken right out of the picture. Dan wasn't going to let me run off on my own and look for a kidnapping victim. He'd send helicopters and a SWAT team after me. And who knew what Alan Davies might do?

And there was at least a reasonable possibility I was wrong. What if I showed up in Oceanside and wound up introducing myself to Chandler Emerson's mistress? That would be…awkward, to say the least.

I went into the garage and looked at my car. There was no way I could drive it in the condition it was in. But my motorcycle was still plugged into the battery charger. I unhooked the wires that fed the battery and checked the bike to be sure it was in neutral, then set the choke to halfway open and tried the ignition switch. The starter grumbled for a moment, but then the engine roared to life. The noise was like hearing an old friend's voice after a long time spent apart. I was amazed to find how much I'd missed it.

I cut back on the choke and let the engine run. It sounded healthy enough. I took a walk around the bike, checking the tires for air pressure and any signs of damage I might have missed. Everything looked good to me. As long as I kept my balance, I should be able to ride with no problem. That didn't mean getting on the bike in my condition was the best idea in the world, but I probably wasn't going to drive into a tree.

I left the bike to run and went back into the house. My helmet was somewhere in my bedroom, if I remembered correctly. I found it in the closet and checked the inside for any opportunistic spiders that might have snuck in there looking for a cozy place to sleep. It was clean, thank god. The only thing worse than finding spiders in there would have been trying to get them out.

My old riding jacket was hanging in the bedroom closet as well. The black leather smelled good to me; one more thing I'd missed more than I ever would have expected. Plus, it made me look like a total badass, which was a bonus.

Back in the kitchen I allowed myself one more swallow of vodka. I needed to drink just enough to keep myself from getting sick in the near future. If I got an attack of the shakes on the bike I was going to crash, and probably crash hard.

Oceanside was a straight shot up I-5. I kept the bike at just under the speed limit and reached the city in less than an hour.

Riding again felt good, but I was glad Emerson's house wasn't located any further north. There was an immigration checkpoint about ten miles up the freeway from my exit, and I didn't want anyone stopping me to take a closer look at what was under my helmet. I didn't know what I smelled like to other people, but it certainly couldn't have been good. Besides, I probably still had chalk in my hair. I'd never taken that shower.

Emerson's second house wasn't difficult to find. I'd have described it as entirely average if anyone asked. It was a ranch-style house that probably dated back to the late 1970's or early 1980's, when about nine out of ten houses built in California had been of that design. This one had a protruding one-car garage on the right-hand side with a late-model Taurus parked in front of the closed retractable door. A stone path led to the front door on the house's left-hand side. Two large windows in front of the house faced the street. From one of them I could see lights were on inside. Someone was definitely home, then. The question was how many someones, and who were they?

I parked on the opposite side of the street, two houses up from Emerson's place. He'd never seen my motorcycle before, of course, but anyone inside who looked out his window might wonder who had parked in front of his house. There was no reason to tip anyone off that I was here. I locked my helmet to the bike's frame and took a deep breath. I could do this. I just needed a look inside the house, that was all. Once I knew what I was going on in there I could leave and call whoever needed to be called.

I tucked my hands in my jacket pockets as I walked across the street and was surprised to feel something metallic in one of them. I pulled it out and saw I'd finally found my cell phone. So that was where it had been. In just about the last place I ever would have looked.

Once I was in front of Emerson's house I took a good look around, checking for any late-night dog walkers or joggers. Nobody was on the sidewalk. Feeling like a thief, I stepped up to the Taurus and took a look inside. There was nothing out of place in there. Then again, what had I really expected to see? Guns? Anna? Of course there was nothing in the car. How had I ever become a detective?

After taking another look around to see if anyone was watching, I sidled up to the house's largest window facing the street and peeked inside. The window had a view of the house's living room. Two heavily tattooed Mexicans were sitting at a folding card table playing dominos. A portable stereo sat on the floor next to the wall, playing music I could only barely hear. There was no other furniture in the living room. Either these two guys had just arrived and were waiting for the moving truck with all of their things to show up, or nobody actually lived here.

One of the men turned his head slightly as if he'd seen me and I ducked out of sight. A breathless moment passed with nothing happening, and I looked in again. Neither of them had appeared to notice me. One of the men was holding his hands up in the air and smiling, as if he'd just scored a domino. Or something. I'd never played dominoes and had no idea how the scoring worked.

I couldn't see any sign of Anna or anyone else in the living room, but I did see something that gave me chills. A shotgun was propped up against the wall near the stereo. So two men had just moved in here, without any furniture or luggage, but they'd brought weapons along. That hardly seemed likely. But buying an empty house to hide your kidnapping victims? I could believe that, although I had to wonder why Emerson had bought the house, rather than just rented one. Maybe he wanted to flip it and make a profit. That seemed like something he'd do. Or he might have been concerned about a pesky landlord stopping by. If he owned the house, he controlled it, along with who could come and go.

I wished, not for the first time in recent days, that I still had my gun. I suddenly felt very naked without it.

I went back to the sidewalk and looked up and down the street. None of the neighbors seemed to have noticed my presence. There were no faces peering out of windows at me, telephones pressed to ears as the police were called. It wouldn't necessarily be a bad thing if the cops showed up to arrest me as a drunken peeping tom, provided I could convince them to take a look inside the house before they hauled me off to jail. But they probably wouldn't bother once they got a whiff of me.

I knew perfectly well that this was the time I should step away from this and call in the cavalry. But I was sure Anna was in the house. I couldn't walk away now. I had to press on. I had to know if she was safe.

A wooden gate was set in a short piece of fence between the end of the garage and the property-line fence to my right. It was too tall for me to see over, but if this was like many suburban California homes, the gate would lead to a path that would go straight to the rear of the house, and most likely a swimming pool and patio area. And if I was lucky, other doors.

I took another look around, then reached over the gate and felt around in the back, hoping it was the kind with a padlock latch near the top. I didn't feel much like climbing over the gate, but I probably could if I needed to. After a moment of fumbling I felt metal. I pressed on it and the gate popped open. Given that nobody really lived here, they'd probably never thought about securing it. Lucky me.

I opened the gate slowly. The hinges were in desperate need of some WD-40, but the men inside had the radio on and were distracted with their game. If I was lucky they weren't hearing any of this.

After another look around, I stepped through the gate and closed it behind me. I didn't bother to latch it. The gate wasn't in any shape to swing open on its own and if I needed to run on my way out of here, leaving it unlatched would buy me a precious second or two.

Once I was invisible to anyone on the street I took a moment to collect myself, surprised to find that I was already breathing hard and starting to sweat. When this was over maybe I'd try to detox myself for a few days. It would be nice to be able to walk for more than a few dozen feet without getting tired.

As I'd suspected, the gate led to a concrete path that ran along the side of the house toward the backyard. A door set immediately to the left of the gate would have to lead into the garage. I pressed my ear against it and listened, but couldn't hear anything coming from inside. I tried the knob. It was unlocked. I wasn't ready to go inside yet, though. I wanted to get a better look around the place first.

Two small windows that I was guessing belonged to bedrooms were set in the wall along the side of the house. They were too high up for me to see through, and would have been too small for me to fit through even if they'd been open and I'd had a ladder.

I crept slowly down the path, wanting to have a look at the back of the house before I did anything else. My footsteps were silent on the concrete, even though my legs were just a little unsteady. One more sip of vodka before I'd left my house would have been a good idea, but it was too late to worry about that now.

A swimming pool about thirty feet long lay just behind the house next to a patio area. The pool was only about one-quarter full and the water was littered with fallen leaves. It was the kind of water you didn't go into unless you wanted to come out with tetanus. Nobody had swum in there in quite some time.

This side of the house had two more windows set into the wall above my head, and then a sliding glass door farther down. Given the light I could see coming from inside, I was willing to bet that the sliding door led into the living room. I thought about going up to it and trying to get another look inside, but decided against it. It was too much of a risk to take just to see the living room from the other side, and if the men spotted me this time, it was going to be considerably harder for me to get away then when I'd been on the street. It had been a while since I'd run anywhere and I doubted I was going to be all that fast, even if I managed to keep from collapsing in exhaustion after a few steps.

I went back to the door that led into the garage and listened at it again. There was nothing but silence from inside. I turned the knob slowly and then pushed the door open about half an inch. I could see only darkness. Relieved, I opened the door wide enough to let a little bit of the light from outside in. I could make out a van parked inside, but that was all. Why on earth hadn't I brought along a flashlight?

The lack of light coming from any other source suggested I could safely turn on the garage lights. At least, that's what I hoped it suggested. I fumbled along the wall until I found a light switch and turned it on, then had to squint against the brightness. The garage was empty except for an older Econoline van. It was the cleanest I'd ever seen a garage.

I spotted the door that led into the house, gauged its distance, and then shut off the light. Leaving the exterior door open gave me just enough light to feel my way along the wall until I came to the interior door. I put my ear up against it and listened, but couldn't hear anything from inside. I tried the door very gently and found it unlocked. That was a relief. I'd picked locks before, but even if I'd had my tools I was fairly clumsy at it. On an exterior door that wouldn't have mattered much, but on an interior door the people inside might well have heard the racket I was making, even over their music, and come to see what was going on.

The door opened inward, which was pretty far from ideal in this situation. I'd have to open the door much farther than I'd have liked to get a look at what was on the other side. It took me a solid minute of slow maneuvering to open the door just enough that I could see it led to a long hallway with two doors on my right-hand side. Those would probably be the bedrooms whose windows I'd seen from outside earlier. Another hall went off to the left just after the bedroom door farthest from me. Judging from how clearly I could hear their music now, that hall would probably go straight to the living room.

I waited a moment, holding my breath, as I thought about what to do. I knew I should leave, but the bedrooms were *right there* in front of me, and Anna could be in one of them. It would take me thirty seconds to look, and then I'd know. Thirty seconds to spot her, go back the way I'd come, and then make the call that would get her out of here. If she wasn't bound, I might even be able to grab her and take her along with me.

The music would make it difficult to hear any movement coming from the living room, but the Mexicans had seemed pretty engrossed in their game and I didn't need much time. Still, if I got caught, I was probably going to get my head blown off.

I crept slowly down the hall toward the first bedroom. It turned out to be entirely empty, without so much as carpet on the floor. One down, one to go.

The second bedroom was similarly devoid of furniture and carpet, but when I saw what was inside I was glad I'd thrown up earlier so I wouldn't feel the need to do so again. A girl of about ten was sitting in the middle of the floor. I recognized Anna Davies from her photos. She was disheveled and dirty and I could see tracks on her face from where she'd been crying. But when she looked up at me her eyes were lifeless, much the way my own appeared to me whenever I looked in the mirror.

Next to Anna on the floor lay the body of her mother. Anna's right wrist had been handcuffed to Heather's ankle, her mother's dead weight keeping her from escaping. Even if Anna managed to move while locked to her mother's body, she wouldn't get very far as long as she had to drag it along with her.

Anna looked down at her mother, then back at me, and I

knew there was no way I was going to leave her to call for help. I knelt down in front of her. "It's all right," I whispered. "I'm going to get you out of here."

I fingered the handcuffs. They weren't police grade; they looked like something that might have been picked up in a sex shop or novelty store. I could probably pop them open with a paperclip or a hairpin, if I could find one. I looked around the room. I didn't need much to work with. Was there anything here I could use?

Anna watched me without curiosity, then her eyes left me and focused on something over my shoulder. I turned around and wasn't entirely surprised to see Chandler Emerson there, pointing a gun at me.

Chapter 21

Emerson kept his gun leveled at my head as I stood up slowly, keeping my hands in view. "Nevada James," he hissed.

"You sick fuck," I said.

He frowned, clearly having expected to hear something else out of me. "What?"

"You left her in here with her mother's dead body?" I asked. One of the Mexicans entered the bedroom and stood just behind Emerson. He'd brought along the shotgun I'd seen earlier. "Just *handcuffed* like this?"

"I…" Emerson started.

"You left her handcuffed to her mother's dead body?" I took a step toward him. "What in the *fuck* is wrong with you?"

"Stop right there," he said. I watched his gun hand, hoping to spot a tremor, but it was as steady as a rock. Chandler Emerson wasn't the small man I'd sized him up as before. He *did* have the steel to pull this off. And more than that, judging from what he'd done to Anna. It wasn't the worst thing I'd ever seen, but it certainly made the list.

"I can't help but notice you're not in Switzerland."

"No," he said. "I'm not."

"And the guys you were supposed to be taking with you?" I nodded at the shotgun-toting Mexican. "These two?"

"No. Those two had an unfortunate accident on the way to the airport." His eyes burned as he glared at me. "You really fouled this up for me, you stupid bitch."

That kind of language hardly seemed necessary. "So it was you all along," I said.

"Quite frankly? I'm surprised it took you this long to figure it out," he said.

"Me, too," I admitted. "But then I've got a pretty serious drinking problem."

"Pity I wasted poor Todd on you," he scoffed. "I'd been saving him for a rainy day, and somehow I got it into my head that you might actually be a threat. If I'd realized how hopeless you really were I'd never have bothered."

"Why kill Heather?" I asked. "Did she try to escape?"

Emerson glanced back at the shotgun-toting Mexican, who managed to look just slightly ashamed of himself. "She tried to fight," the lawyer said. "But it was just delaying the inevitable. They were always going to die."

"But why?" I asked. "Because you helped get them out of the condo? There were easier ways you could have kidnapped them and they'd never have seen your face," I said. "Send this guy to grab them in a parking lot, or…"

Emerson smirked at me condescendingly. I'd missed something.

"Oh," I said. "But you could never have spent the ransom as long as Davies was still alive. 'Where did you get that new Ferrari, Chandler?' 'Oh, I won the lottery.' So he has to die, too."

"Quite right," he said. His hand tightened on the gun. "Goodbye, Ms. James."

"Who are you framing for it?"

He lowered the gun slightly. "What?"

"Who are you setting Davies up against? *Los Zetas? La Familia?*"

"Why would you possibly care about that?"

"I don't know," I shrugged. "I just love mysteries so much."

Emerson lowered the gun to his side. It hardly mattered when his friend had a shotgun in his hands. I wasn't going to have a chance to rush him. "My god, you're drunk *right now*, aren't you?"

"A little," I admitted. "Not nearly enough."

Emerson shared a disgusted glance with the Mexican, who rolled his eyes at me. Asshole. "*Sinaloa,*" Emerson said.

I nodded. "Makes sense."

"Oh, I'm so glad you approve."

"Davies doesn't have the resources to fight the *Sinaloa* Cartel," I said. "They're way out of his league. They'd get to him in…what, a day? Two?" I laughed. "My god, it really would be the end of *Scarface* up there."

"He'd die in a blaze of glory," Emerson said. "And I'd be on a plane to Fiji, with nobody the wiser."

I snickered and Emerson scowled at me. "What? What did I miss?"

"It's not that," I said. "You said, 'the wiser.' I haven't heard anybody say that since…" I thought about it. "I've never actually heard anyone say that."

"Well, I'm glad you got some amusement out of this before your death. Unfortunately, little Anna is going to be stuck in here with two bodies now, but not for much longer. She'll be good for one more phone call, I think, and then this will all be over."

"You're an even bigger asshole than I thought you were," I said. "And don't get me wrong, I thought you were a pretty serious asshole in the first place."

He raised the pistol. "And you're a stupid dead bitch."

"No," I said. "Bad idea."

"Really? And why is that?"

"Because you've only got one murder on you now," I said. "Heather. Those two other guys that you killed, somehow I doubt they're ever going to be found. You might get charged with accessory for Todd's death, but I doubt it'll stick. So one murder. You'll get life for that. But you kill an ex-cop and a kid, the prosecutor is going to ask for the death penalty, and he'll get it. The jury won't even need to leave the room to deliberate."

Emerson rolled his eyes. "You seem to have forgotten the

part where I'm on a plane to Fiji."

"You'll never make it to the airport," I said. He frowned in confusion. "You mind?" I pointed at my jacket, and when he nodded reached into it slowly. The Mexican raised his shotgun at me. "Hey, hey!" I said. "Nice and slow. Don't shoot." I took my cell phone out of my pocket and showed it to them.

Emerson's brow wrinkled. "So? Do you think I'm really going to stand here while you call 911?"

"You're kidding right?" I asked. "Do you really think I'd be stupid enough to walk in here without calling the cops *first*?" I grinned. "I called SDPD the minute I stepped onto your property."

The Mexican spun on his heel and darted out of the room. Emerson turned his head to watch the other man leave. I heard raised voices shouting at each other in Spanish, and then the front door banged open. They were gone.

"Yeah," I said. "That just happened. You might want to go with them."

Emerson looked back at me, eyes wide. His plan was falling apart right in front of him. "They'll be here any minute," I said. "*Go!*"

He raised the pistol. "Bitch!"

"Ah, ah," I said. "Death penalty. Is it really worth it just to kill me?"

Murder in his eyes, Emerson turned and fled.

I waited until I was sure he was gone, then allowed myself a sigh of relief. My cell phone was still in my hand. Out of curiosity, I hit the power button. Somehow the battery had held up and the phone switched on, but there was no service. I hadn't paid the bill in months. At some point Verizon had cut me off. Luckily for me and Anna, Emerson had fallen for my bluff. That had just saved our lives.

At some point during his escape Emerson might well notice that police cars were not racing toward his house. I didn't know how long that might take, but I needed to find a phone before it did. Odds were he'd hooked up phone service here when he'd had the power turned on. If not, I'd go to a neighbor.

I knelt down in front of Anna. "I'll be right back, okay?" I wanted to take her with me, but I didn't have a way to get the handcuffs off of her and I was afraid to take the time to look. I'd find a way to do that after I'd called for help.

A single tear rolled down the girl's cheek. I sighed. This poor kid was going to be in therapy for the rest of her life. If I'd had any social skills at all I'd have been able to say something comforting, but what was there to say? "Sorry you've been handcuffed here next to your mother's corpse?" There was nothing I could ever say that would make her feel better.

Except maybe this. "I'm going to make a phone call, and then I'll take you home," I told her, putting a hand on her shoulder. "Your dad is waiting for you."

Chapter 22

I found a phone in the living room and made the call. The Oceanside cops showed up five minutes later. If Emerson had ever figured out I was bluffing, he didn't show up at the house to check. I doubted I'd ever see him again.

I'd lied about taking Anna home. The cops got her out of the handcuffs, and then the EMTs put her in an ambulance and drove her away. I had to stay behind to give a statement to the cops. Then I got one of them to tell me where Anna was going, and I got on my bike and went after them.

Anna was in an examination room when I got to the hospital. I went to the nurse's station and told them I was her stepmother. One of the nurses told me my husband was already in the room with her. I thanked her and took a seat in the waiting area out front.

After a time Alan Davies came out and spotted me. He crossed over to where I was sitting. "I thought you'd be here," he said.

"How is she?"

"No physical trauma," Davies said, sitting down. "She's dehydrated and they didn't give her much to eat. Tell me what happened."

I told him. He took it fairly well. At one point he got up and punched a vending machine hard enough that it probably registered on the Richter scale, but I hadn't liked that vending machine much anyway.

"Find Chandler for me," he said, sitting down again.

"No," I said. "Find him yourself."

"I'll pay you…"

"You're going to pay me anyway," I said. "You got your daughter back."

Davies sighed. "Yes," he said. "Yes, I did. Fine. I'll find him myself. There is nowhere he can run that I won't find him."

"That's secondary," I said.

"What?"

"Your priority right now needs to be your daughter."

"I know my daughter is a priority!"

"You don't understand," I said. "You saw that look she was giving you before?"

He frowned. "She didn't look at me much at all."

"You don't recognize it," I said, "but I've been there and I know what's happening to her. She is going to need serious therapy. Starting tomorrow. I know someone in San Diego who is good. If she doesn't work with kids, she'll know who does." I couldn't remember if Molly was practicing at all anymore, but she'd be the first person I called in the morning.

"Okay."

"Eventually she's going to need to talk to you. You probably won't like what she says. Listen anyway."

"I will."

"She's young. Kids are resilient. But what she's been through, it was bad. You need to understand this is a process, and it will probably be a long one." I looked up and saw someone I knew coming toward us. "And you better go back in her room right now."

Davies looked up. Dan Evans was marching up the hall. He didn't look like he was coming to tell us a new joke he'd just heard.

"Go," I said.

Davies got up and went back into Anna's room, nodding once at Dan as he passed. Dan didn't nod back. He came to stand directly in front of me, hands at his sides.

"Hi, boss," I said.

"Hi."

"What's up?"

"I had a really interesting call from Oceanside PD," he said. "They told me…"

"Not now."

"*What?*"

"I can't do this now. I just can't, Dan. Can we talk about it later?" I looked up at him. "Please?"

He hesitated. "We *will* talk about it later. At length."

"Fine," I said. "Sit down."

He sat. For a while we didn't say anything. I really wanted him to hold my hand, but there was no way I was ever going to reach out, and if he had tried I'd probably have just pulled away.

For a while we watched people go back and forth, into rooms and out of them, up and down the halls. "Are you okay?" Dan asked finally.

"No," I said. "I'm really not."

Chapter 23

Three days later Dan and I were standing on the Ocean Beach pier. We'd walked out to the little café at the far end and bought lobster tacos and sodas. My treat. I could afford it now. Alan Davies had been true to his word. I wasn't going to need to worry about money for a long time.

It was a windy day, partly cloudy and about seventy degrees. In other words, it was just like every other day in San Diego. I'd always loved the city, but damned if I wouldn't have liked a little variety in the weather now and then.

I'd only had one drink this morning and found it was enough to keep me from shaking, at least so far. I didn't feel like I was about to vomit at any moment, either. It was a different kind of feeling. Good, yes. But different. I'd even showered, put on clean clothes, and brushed out my hair.

A chunk of meat fell out of Dan's taco and landed on the wooden planks below. "God *damn* it," he said.

"I hate it when that happens."

Dan eyed the fallen lobster meat for just a moment too long and I knew what he was thinking. "Really?" I asked.

"Nah," he said. "Probably get hepatitis."

"You'd be lucky if that was all you got."

"Yeah." He bit into what was left of his taco and chewed it thoughtfully.

"Your plan failed," I said.

"What?"

"You thought working a case was going to save me," I said. "I'm not saved. So there."

"I don't know," he shrugged.

"What, I *am* saved? I had vodka for breakfast."

"You look better," Dan said.

"Really?"

"Don't get me wrong, you still look pretty sick. But you looked half-dead when you walked into my office the other morning. I figure we bought you a little time. I may not have to speak at your funeral until *next* month, which is an improvement."

"You're hilarious."

"I wasn't kidding."

I flipped him off and he nearly smiled. Nearly.

"I heard from Alan Davies," I said.

"I figured you would have. How's the girl?"

"She's barely spoken, apparently."

"I imagine she's going to need a lot of therapy."

"Her father is the Mafia and her mother was murdered in front of her. I would think therapy will be a recurring theme in her life."

"Yeah. What about Emerson?"

"He's in the wind. If he's smart he's in a hole halfway around the world right now. Davies is never going to stop looking for him."

"Well, fuck him anyway," Dan said. I looked at him in surprise and he shrugged. "If anyone asks, I said Chandler Emerson should be brought to justice, of course."

"Of course."

"And what about you?" he asked.

I watched a group of pelicans feeding in the gentle waves next to the pier. "I honestly don't know."

He nodded. "If you wanted to come back..."

"No."

"Think about it a little before you say that."

"I don't have to think about it," I said. "You were right to fire me. I was mad at you about it, but you were right. I was in no shape to be a cop after I got out of the hospital."

"That was a long time ago."

"Not long enough," I said. "I'm still..." I thought about what Molly had said to me before. "I'm broken."

"You're not broken."

"My thinking is broken, then," I said. "When they were

trying to put my brain back together, some things wound up in the wrong place."

"Okay."

"I'm fucking *nuts*, honestly."

"I wouldn't go that far."

"I would. And then there's…" I stopped. He waited for me to say it. "I'm an alcoholic."

He didn't say anything. He wasn't the type to say "I told you so."

"It was getting to be a problem before the Laughing Man," I admitted. "But it didn't get out of control until I went after him and…damn it, Dan, he was always a step ahead of me. Taunting me. He was beating me and that was how I coped with it."

"And now?"

"I don't know. I may get another therapist."

"Sarah tells me you were going to go to an A.A. meeting."

"I did."

"How did that go?"

"What's said there stays there," I told him sagely. He didn't need to know what I'd really gone there for.

"Are you going to go back?"

I intended to say something sarcastic, but what came out of my mouth was, "I'll think about it." I blinked in surprise. Where had *that* come from?

"Okay," he said. He looked as surprised as I felt.

We turned to the water and watched the waves roll in for a while. "It's going to be nice today," he said.

"It's nice here every day."

"You know what I mean."

"Yeah," I said. "I do."

Chapter 24

I'd walked out to the pier to meet Dan, and refused his offer to drive me home. It was nice out, and I found I wanted the fresh air. I'd spent so much time in my house in the past few years I'd forgotten how good an ocean breeze could feel.

Back home I decided that I'd earned a nap. But on the way to my bedroom I made a detour into the kitchen and took a fresh bottle of vodka down from the cabinet above the sink. I cracked it open and poured an inch of it into a clean glass. Then I put the bottle down, picked up the glass, and just looked at it.

By any logic in the world I shouldn't drink it. But this wasn't about logic. It was about a need that would have been impossible to explain to anyone who hadn't experienced it. And I wasn't sure I really understood it, myself. Was it so I'd stop feeling things for a while? Was it a security blanket? Was it just part of who I was?

I sniffed the liquid in the glass as if that was going to answer the question for me. The thought of actually drinking it depressed me. It was like wearing clothes you found in the dumpster because you couldn't afford anything else. It was walking in the ditch because the paved road was, for some unexplainable reason, too frightening.

Fuck it. I took a sip and swallowed.

Instantly I felt both revolted and panicky. Why had I done that? But the question was made moot a moment later as my body rebelled against the liquor and I vomited it up into the sink. Bits of lobster taco and vodka splashed against the basin. I had to hold onto the counter to keep upright until the retching was over, and then long enough to catch my breath again.

Drinking was definitely out today. I poured the rest of my glass into the sink. My body just couldn't handle it. Maybe I'd feel differently after I'd slept a little.

I picked up the bottle of vodka, looked at it for a moment, then upended it over the sink and watched as the liquid ran down the drain. I was never going to drink this shit. Maybe I'd quit drinking. And maybe I'd just switch to good Scotch, but my cheap vodka days were definitely over.

I went into the cabinet and found another bottle, which I emptied the same as I had the first. Then I looked through the rest of the cabinets and cleaned everything with alcohol out of them. I even found an unopened bottle of Schnapps and regarded it with surprise. When had I bought *this* shit? I hated Schnapps. It went down the drain with everything else.

All of the empties wound up filling two Hefty bags. I bundled them up, tied the tops, and then started toward the front door. I'd put them in the dumpster outside so I wouldn't have to put up with the lingering smell of cheap booze, and then I was going to clean the hell out of this place. Not just picking up garbage this time, but a real cleaning, with Lysol and bleach and whatever else I had under the sink. My house hadn't had a proper cleaning in years. Did my vacuum even work anymore? I had no idea when I'd turned it on last. I might have to go buy a new one. Maybe I'd even call a carpet cleaning company in. The place sure as hell needed it.

I was rounding the corner into the living room with the garbage sacks in my hands when I saw Chandler Emerson coming toward me, eyes filled with rage. I dropped the bags but didn't have the time to react as he pressed a stun gun to my chest and hit the trigger. A blast of pain exploded throughout my body and I fell to the floor, twitching uncontrollably. My nervous system was shot. I couldn't move.

Emerson stood over me, breathing hard. I didn't know how long the effects of a stun gun would last. Ten minutes? Fifteen? In any case, I was going to be incapacitated for at least a few minutes. If he didn't blast me again, that was.

The lawyer put the stun gun in his pocket and took hold of my wrists. He began dragging me along the floor. I couldn't make my head turn to see where we were going, but it seemed like we were heading for the kitchen.

He grunted and moaned as he dragged me. The man obviously wasn't in great shape, but unfortunately I didn't weigh very much. If only my addiction had been to chocolate cake, this whole thing might be going in a very different direction.

Emerson lugged me slowly through the kitchen and into the dining room. My body was still twitching when he laid me out next to the dining room table, but I was able to make my hand flex. Emerson saw it. "No, you don't!" he said. He took the stun gun out of his pocket and blasted me in the chest again, setting off a new round of pain and twitching. Then, with a kind a maniacal glee in his eyes, he pressed the stun gun against my cheek and pressed the trigger a third time. I was already in so much pain I nearly didn't feel the new shock, but I decided if I lived through this I was going to beat the hell out of him before I called the police.

Emerson put the stun gun down on the dining room table and then bent over to grab me under my arms. He grunted loudly as he hoisted me up into a chair and propped me up so I couldn't slide off of it. Then he turned and left the room. I couldn't turn my head quickly enough to follow him, but I heard him go into the living room and then my front door opened. A moment passed in silence and I tried to get my body to do something, *anything*, but it refused to cooperate. I knew Emerson was coming back, and I probably wasn't going to like what he'd be bringing with him.

The front door opened and closed again. Emerson reappeared in the dining room with a red toolbox that still had the price tag attached. He'd probably bought it this morning. That was unexpected. I'd figured he was out getting tools to cut me up with, not actual tools. Maybe he was going to do a little carpentry and just didn't want me getting in the way. Or maybe I didn't want to know what was in the toolbox.

Emerson opened the toolbox and removed a roll of duct tape. He peeled the end of the tape away from the roll and then began circling me, wrapping the tape in tight circles around my arms as he secured me to the chair. I was in no danger of falling off of it now. And I certainly wouldn't be able to move anytime soon.

In the end he used far more tape than he needed to, probably thinking using too much was better than too little. He had that much right, at least. After using nearly the entire roll, he took a box cutter out of the toolbox and cut the remainder away. He patted the tape down, making sure it was secure against my body. Then he stepped back to admire his handiwork. "How do you like that, you fucking bitch?" he asked.

I tried to tell him to go fuck himself, but my lips were numb and I sounded like someone mumbling in their sleep. He got enough of it to understand what I'd said, though, and punched me in the face hard enough to make my teeth rattle. My vision filled with stars.

I had little chance of being rescued, I realized. Dan had no reason to come and check on me, and it wasn't like I had any friends who might stop by to say hello. Emerson could kill me here and it could be days before anyone knew I was even missing. Days, or weeks, maybe.

Emerson looked at the box cutter in his hand, frowned at it, then went into his toolbox again and came out with a miniature blowtorch, the kind home cooks wanting to try something fancy used to sear a crust on a crème brûlée. He clicked the trigger and a blue flame about an inch long appeared at the nozzle. He held the trigger down for a moment so I could get a good look at it, then shut the flame off.

"I'll wait until the shock wears off," he said, nodding at me. "You really should feel this after what you've done to me."

I concentrated on making my mouth work. "Fuck you," I said. There. That had actually sounded pretty good.

"Goddamn whore," Emerson said. "You ruined my life. I

was almost done with him. I was so close. You should have just crawled back into the gutter you came out of and died."

I flexed my hands. My twitching had stopped and I could feel my nervous system slowly switching itself back on, like someone checking the lights in a building after a blackout. In another minute I'd be back at a hundred percent. Not that it would matter much. I wasn't going anywhere as long as I was taped to this chair.

"What do you think is going to happen here?" I asked, forcing my words to come out slowly and clearly. "You're wasting time. You should be running."

"Where am I going to go?" Emerson asked, his voice plaintive. "My assets are frozen. The roads and airports are being watched. If the police don't find me, Alan will. He'll skin me alive for what I've done."

Good, I wanted to say, but maybe I could still talk my way out of this. "So you just came over here to get revenge on me? Think about this. What's your next move?"

He shrugged. "I don't know. I don't care anymore."

I thought it over, trying to look more incapacitated than I actually was to buy some extra time. "Go to Mexico."

"What?"

"Mexico. It's easy. Get on the trolley and take it to San Ysidro. Get off at the last stop and it's a five-minute walk to the border."

He scowled at me. "But the Border Patrol…"

"Have you ever gone into Mexico from San Ysidro? There is no checkpoint to go through. You walk through a turnstile and you're in Tijuana. Nobody gives a shit about you going over there. Coming back is what's hard, and you're never coming back."

Emerson looked like he was actually considering it for a moment, but then he glared at me. "You really think I'm going to go to Mexico and live with those...those *beaners*?"

"Well, you probably shouldn't say that to them," I told him. "It's really racist."

Emerson clicked the blowtorch on. "I think you're ready," he said. "What should we start with?" He brought the blowtorch close to my head, near enough that I could feel its heat. "Your ears? I think we should start with your ears."

He leaned in close. I took a deep breath and clenched my teeth. I didn't want him to hear me scream. I didn't have any illusions that I wouldn't, of course, but I hoped I'd be able to hold out for a minute or two.

I felt the other presence before I saw him. One moment I was waiting for Emerson to burn me and then the hairs on the back of my neck stood up and I knew *he* was here. God help me, I actually opened my mouth to warn Emerson, but it was too late. I saw a shadow move behind the lawyer, then a gloved hand appeared and clapped itself firmly against Emerson's forehead. Another hand appeared, this one holding a straight razor, and opened the lawyer's throat wide in one swift motion. Blood erupted from Emerson's neck like a volcano, much of it splattering onto my face and hair. The lawyer's eyes bulged and he made one quick, wet choking noise as he clutched at his throat, but it was over. The hand on his forehead released him and he crumpled to the ground, dropping the blowtorch as he fell. Without him to hold the trigger, the flame clicked off harmlessly. I was left facing his killer, who held the bloody straight razor at his side as he looked down at me.

The last time I'd seen the Laughing Man he'd been dressed for battle, a mess of leather and body armor that had made him look like a cyberpunk street hockey player. Today he wore jeans and a grey hoodie. He wouldn't have gotten a second look out on the street except for the Greek theatre mask he wore. The mask was painted in solid white, its mouth open in a wide laugh that was probably supposed to look joyful. It looked demonic to me, maybe because I knew a monster was on its other side. He'd worn the same mask three years ago, during our first confrontation. The Laughing Man had cleaned it in the interim. The last time I'd seen it it had been colored with my blood.

The mask covered his entire face, except for his piercing blue eyes. I remembered the eyes, too. I'd remember them until the day I died.

A small slit was carefully concealed in the mask's mouth so he could speak. It had the added effect of amplifying every breath he took. His breathing now was as calm as if he'd been sleeping. I'd have been willing to bet that his pulse rate hadn't increased even a beat while he'd slaughtered Emerson. That had meant no more to him than swatting an insect.

I strained at the duct tape for one brief moment before giving up. It was hopeless. I had no chance of escaping. At least not before he cut my throat, too.

The Laughing Man watched me for a moment, his head cocked just slightly. Then he knelt down and turned Emerson's face toward himself. He went to work with the straight razor. I didn't have to wonder what he was doing. The Laughing Man would remove the lips, then cut away the skin covering Emerson's teeth, going all the way back to where his jaw hinged. When he was finished Emerson would be left with the same grotesque grin the Laughing Man carved into each of his victims. The last time I'd seen that mutilation it had been on the faces of the two little girls I'd been so desperately trying to save three years ago. I had already been teetering on the edge of madness back then, and that was all it had taken to push me over the edge.

It wasn't going to happen this time. I wouldn't let it.

I turned my face away as the Laughing Man cut on Emerson, the only sound in the room that of flesh being sliced and tossed away. When it was done, the Laughing Man took a moment to inspect his work. Satisfied, he heaved Emerson up into the chair at the head of the dining room table. He pushed the chair in neatly and moved Emerson's body into a position that suggested he was alive and well. He was making a still-life, I realized. Emerson would have looked like a man sitting down to dinner, mouth open in laughter. The Laughing Man didn't have enough bodies to make a family, of course, except for me. He could make Emerson a wife, if he wanted to. Was that his plan? Was this how I was going to die?

The Laughing Man went into the kitchen and began to search my cabinets. It took him a few trips, but he eventually managed to set two places at the table with plates, silverware, napkins, and drinking glasses. I hadn't seen some of those things in years. How long had it been since I'd set my own dinner table? Had I *ever* set my own dinner table?

When he was finished the Laughing Man turned to me and heaved my chair around so I was facing the table. Then he began sliding it forward. It was difficult work, given that I was taped to the chair, but slowly and surely he got me into position across from Emerson at the table. Here we were, just sitting down to enjoy our imaginary dinner together. It might have looked like that to an observer at first glance, before they got close enough to see the horrible truth.

The table set and all of his pieces in position, the Laughing Man took a third chair at the table and sat down. He looked at me expectantly.

I looked back at him. "Not your best work," I said.

He raised his gloved left palm in a "what can you do" expression. His right hand toyed with the straight razor, snapping it open and closed. I watched him as calmly as I could. He could kill me if he wanted to. I couldn't stop him. But he was never going to see fear from me. Never.

What was he waiting for?

Finally he bent forward toward me, just slightly. "Did you enjoy it?" he asked softly. He had a tenor voice, nearly musical, both amplified and just slightly distorted by the mask. It was exactly as I remembered it from our last confrontation. That voice had haunted my nightmares.

I stared at him. "What did you say?"

The Laughing Man sighed quietly. "Your case." He nodded at Emerson. "The game. Did you enjoy it?"

That was what this was about? He wanted to talk? Like we were old friends who had just gotten together to catch up?

I supposed that in a sick way, it was very much like that.

Well, why *not* tell him? It wasn't like I had anything better to do.

"I did," I admitted. "I honestly did." I shook my head. "It was good to feel like I was doing something worthwhile."

"Good," the Laughing Man said. "I'm glad."

"I knew you were watching me," I said. "All the things you sent me in the last three years, the cards, the notes. I knew you were out there. I never realized how close you were…"

"I was waiting," the Laughing Man cut me off. He sounded very nearly mournful now. "I've missed *our* game, and I've been very patient with you, Nevada James. Very patient, but…" He raised the straight razor, looked at it meaningfully, then looked back at me. "Now I have to ask you. Are you back?"

I understood him now. If I said no he'd cut my throat and be done with it. All of this would be over. My pain, my nightmares, my shame. It would be so easy and I probably wouldn't even feel it. One slice and I'd be done.

And he'd go find another playmate.

I'd have been lying if I said I wasn't tempted. Or if I said I didn't want it. I'd been killing myself for the last three years, hadn't I? Why not let him finish me off?

Because it wasn't going to be him that did it. When our story was over, it would be me standing over this fucker's body. Not the other way around. He didn't *get* to kill me. When I died it would be on my own terms, not his.

I looked him in the eyes. "I'm back," I said.

The Laughing Man lowered the razor and stood up. He crossed over to where I sat and put a hand on my shoulder. As he looked down at me I saw his eyes were almost gentle now. "Finally," he said. The relief in his voice was audible.

"Cut this tape off me and I'll show you how back I am," I offered. I knew he'd never do it, of course. That wasn't how the Laughing Man played the game.

I heard him chuckle softly through the mask. Then he straightened up and went into the kitchen where the cordless phone sat in its cradle. He picked it up and brought it over to where I sat, clicked it on, and dialed 911. Then he put the phone down on the table in front of me, patted me once on the shoulder, and walked away. I heard him open and close my front door. In ten minutes he could be having coffee on the other side of the city and nobody would have any idea of the monster that was in their midst, hiding in plain sight.

The emergency operator's voice was barely audible through the phone's speaker. "My name is Nevada James," I said. "I need help." I didn't know if she could understand me or not, but it didn't matter. A police cruiser would be dispatched in under a minute. The cops would be here in five more. They'd break in and find me, and see what the Laughing Man had done. After three years in the darkness, he was finally back. The Laughing Man was back.

And so was I.

"I am back," I said out loud. "Goddamn right I'm back."

Game on.

ABOUT THE AUTHOR

Matthew Storm lives in Anchorage, Alaska.

www.ingramcontent.com/pod-product-compliance
Lightning Source LLC
Chambersburg PA
CBHW061147170626
46809CB00003B/1020